"So, what do you want? A straight orgasm, or the works?"

Will pressed the telephone receiver more tightly to his ear, blood pooling in his loins. This woman was going to be the death of him. "Wha—whatever you think is best."

"Okay," Rowan replied. "I'm really glad you called. I've been lonely, lying here in this big old bed."

Her voice was husky, rife with the promise of a wet dream. Suddenly Will didn't want Rowan playing this phone-sex-operator role—he wanted her to participate, to sigh and moan for real. To be as turned on as he was...

Will pitched his voice lower to match hers. Payback was going to be sweet. "Lonely, huh? Maybe I can do something about that. What if I were to kiss the sweet curve of your neck, trace my fingers over your breasts...?"

A sharp gasp on the other end told Will he'd made his point. "Then I'd kiss my way down your belly, hook your legs over my shoulders and taste you," he continued. "And once you'd melted, I'd slide into your heat, over and over, until you came again." His breathing grew ragged, snapping under the strain of their sexy wordplay.

"Can you feel me there, Rowan?" he whispered. "Can you feel me?"

Dear Reader,

Like many of my ideas, the creative nudge behind this book came from a trip to my hairdresser's. (Honestly, so many ideas have come out of that shop, I've begun to wonder if my muse isn't addicted to hair chemicals, color foils and bleach.) Anyway, I picked up a magazine and read an article about an unemployed woman who turned to phone sex to make ends meet, and while the color lifted from my ever-darkening hair, the creative juices started flowing.

When budget cuts put high school teacher Rowan Crosswhite out of her job, she comes up with an ingenious way to make ends meet—she installs her own 1-900 phone sex line. It's safe, it's harmless and most important, it's profitable. And when Will Foster comes onto the scene, it becomes deliciously wicked fun.

I hope you enjoy the heat, humor and heart in Rowan and Will's story. For more information about past and upcoming books, be sure to check out my Web site, www.booksbyRhondaNelson.com.

Happy reading,

Rhonda Nelson

Books by Rhonda Nelson

1-900-LOVER

Rhonda Nelson

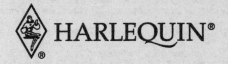

HARLEQUIN®

TORONTO • NEW YORK • LONDON
AMSTERDAM • PARIS • SYDNEY • HAMBURG
STOCKHOLM • ATHENS • TOKYO • MILAN • MADRID
PRAGUE • WARSAW • BUDAPEST • AUCKLAND

This one's for you, Granny. For panty-hose wigs and
Martian hats, paper dolls and peanut butter sandwiches.
For countless hours of undivided attention, tight hugs,
fishing trips and sewing lessons. For invaluable advice,
unwavering support and unconditional love.
You're the best, and I love you dearly.

ISBN 0-373-79162-3

1-900-LOVER

www.eHarlequin.com

Printed in U.S.A.

1

"WHAT AM I WEARING?" Rowan Crosswhite echoed into the phone, her voice artfully pitched to a breathy sultry purr. Grimacing, she used the hem of her T-shirt and her frayed denim cutoffs to clean the majority of the potting soil from her hands, then took up her watering can. "I'm wearing a black leather bustier, fishnet hose and stiletto heels."

The fabricated description lacked originality, yes, but thus far in her experience in the phone sex business, she'd learned that any imaginative effort she put into her descriptions *wasn't* appreciated. So why bother?

When Rowan had first considered selling phone sex, she'd worried about being appropriately creative, about fabricating a believable performance for the men who dialed her number. She'd even called a couple of 1-900 numbers for research purposes because being prepared was the keystone to any successful venture, and her near-manic obsession with doing everything to the absolute best of her ability—even something as seedy as being a phone sex operator—had prevented her from doing otherwise.

The research had been a wasted effort and she'd worried needlessly about conjuring a suitable performance.

In fact, ironically, she'd learned the less said the better. Rowan rolled her eyes. Hell, all she really had to do was gasp, wince and moan—easy to do, particularly when one was, say, cleaning the toilet or weeding a flower bed—and the guys, thank God, took care of the rest. One of the many advantages of phone sex.

And, surprisingly, there were many.

First of all—most importantly—it was safe. There was no risk of abuse or disease, and if a guy freaked her out, all she had to do was sever the connection and block the number. She mentally shrugged. Simple enough. Furthermore, and equally important given her recent unfortunate circumstances, it was *lucrative.* At $3.99 a minute, where the average call hovered around the twelve-minute mark, that was roughly $240 an hour. Her lips twitched. Considerably more than her previous job as a high-school science teacher.

Just a year shy of tenure, Rowan had been one

of the unlucky souls left unemployed by deep state budget cuts. Her boss at Middleton High had promised that as soon as the funds were available, she'd be under contract again.

Regrettably, until then, more panting, moaning and wincing would be in order—and the more dramatic the better—otherwise she'd ultimately starve and, much to the detriment of her heavily padded thighs, she liked food entirely too much to go hungry.

Since she'd been paying off student loans and attending night school to get her master's degree, Rowan had been caught with a grand total of $633 in savings, even less in checking and nothing— aside from a 1962 Chevrolet Corvette that had belonged to her father, and for which she would prostitute herself in the literal sense to keep if need be—of any value to sell.

She did substitute teaching when she could, but that income hadn't been enough, or even dependable, for that matter. Then she'd read an article about a woman who, in similar circumstances, had morphed herself into a phone sex entrepreneur, and the rest had been history. She'd weighed the advantages and disadvantages, deemed it a good temporary choice, then installed her line and invested in a good mobile headset.

This freed up her hands and allowed her to

do the things that she really loved—gardening,
stained glass and metal-working. *Tinkering,* according to her father. Her shoulders sagged with
disappointment. Initially, she'd tried to make ends
meet by selling her garden art, but unfortunately—
and this thoroughly baffled her—no one seemed
to get her style. Rowan cast a glance around her
eclectic garden—whimsical metalwork, stained-glass whirligigs, antique roses, bulbs and vines—
and swallowed a despondent sigh. Screw 'em, she
thought, the tasteless traditional cads. *She* was an
artiste. Her garden thrived and made her happy,
which when one really thought about it, was all
that mattered anyway.

A stuttered breath hissed across the line, cut
through her musings. "Wh—what about your
panties? What do they look like?"

Rowan glanced at her watch. She'd had this guy
on the phone for eight minutes. Time to finish up.
She had some impatiens to transplant, and her
roses were looking a little droopy.

"I don't wear panties," she lied breathlessly.
"They…constrict."

Predictably, the line worked. A garbled groan
and the telltale whine of a zipper echoed into her ear.

She lowered her voice. "Can I tell you a secret,
Jeff?" she asked, purposely using his name. It
played into the whole *say-my-name, who's-your-*

daddy mentality. Sheesh. Men were pathetically predictable.

"S-sure."

"Sometimes…when I'm alone…I like to touch myself." She barely suppressed a snigger. Rowan Crosswhite, former high-school science teacher turned kinky phone sex queen.

Another broken hiss sounded. "Are you— Are you touching yourself now?"

"Oh, I want to, Jeff. Do you want me to?"

"Oh, God, yes."

"Then I should probably lie down." Rowan affected a dramatic wince. "My sheets are cool…especially since I'm so *hot.*" That wasn't a complete lie. It *was* hot. And humid, she thought pulling her tank top away from her chest, a vain effort to circulate a little air beneath her shirt.

A harsh breath stuttered across the line. "How hot are you?"

"I'm on fire, Jeff. I'm imagining that you're touching me. Can I touch you?"

"Yes."

Thirty seconds later it was over. She was thirty-six dollars richer and her sheets were still clean. Honestly, if a woman was going to use her body for profit, phone sex was definitely the way to go. In all seriousness, Rowan knew there were some people who would criticize her choice of temporary employment, but she'd used her own morality meter when making the decision. As far as she was concerned, she was providing a harmless form of entertainment. She simply played a part, catered to men's fantasies from a comfortable distance. No harm, no foul. It was a practical business arrangement, one that benefited her, kept food in the fridge and the power on.

She waited until his breathing slowed before she spoke again. "I've enjoyed talking with you, Jeff. Call me again, anytime."

Jeff exhaled a long, satisfied breath. "You can count on it." He paused. "Hey, as long as you're still there, do you mind if I ask you a quick question?"

"Sure. Go ahead." This was common. Men frequently asked her for all kinds of advice. Everything from how to remove stains, to what brand of fabric softener did she prefer. She didn't mind. It was their dime, after all. *Cha-ching.*

She'd even had a teenage boy call—she'd taught enough of them to recognize the pubescent squeaking croak—and, after she'd neatly avoided the sex issue, she'd ended up tutoring him in science. He'd contacted her several times during one week, then the calls had abruptly ceased. She'd been tempted to give him her home number, but Caller ID and cross-referencing had prevented the impulse. What she did on her own time wasn't anyone's business, but she didn't think Middleton's Mississippi Bible Belt board of education would agree. She'd fully expected a call from an outraged parent, but so far nothing had come of it, and she sincerely hoped nothing did.

"I've got a date tonight," the caller said, "and I really want to impress this girl. What do you think? Burger King or McDonald's?"

Rowan rolled her eyes. Her clients, the poor fools. No wonder they could never get laid in the traditional sense. "Wow her," she told him flatly. "Head for the border."

"Taco Bell?" A thoughtful hum, then, "An even better choice. Thanks."

"No problem." She chuckled under her breath and disconnected. Just in the nick of time, too, Rowan thought, as she watched her elderly neighbor, Ida Holcomb, amble unsteadily across her backyard toward Rowan's fence.

Rowan rented the small guest house, which was located at the rear of Ida's property, from the older lady. The white frame house was small, but two-storied with full, sweeping porches on both levels. It was the mini-version of Ida's grand antebellum home and, for what it lacked in modern convenience, it more than made up for in character.

There was only one plug-in in the bathroom, and the pipes invariably froze in the winter, but the ten-foot ceilings lent an airy mood to the house, and the crown molding, fireplace, and hardwood floors had been handcrafted with a quality of workmanship which couldn't be duplicated much less found in today's power-tool, particle-board world. The small greenhouse, workshop and attached garden had made it the perfect choice for Rowan.

When Rowan lost her job, Ida had sacrificed part of the rent in exchange for errands and personal services. Rowan did Ida's grocery shopping, took her to and from the hairdresser's, paid her bills and whatnot. She plucked her eyebrows—not that there were that many left because Ida had been part of a generation where having *no* eyebrows was fashionable—and stoically—*miserably*—rendered the occasional pedicure. Her gaze involuntarily moved to Ida's slowly-approaching slippered feet and she quelled a shudder. In Rowan's opinion, there was nothing remotely attractive about feet, and there was something downright *yuck* about knobby, gnarled old-people feet.

Ick.

For all of that, however, she'd nonetheless grown very fond of her neighbor. Her grandparents had passed away when she was small, and her parents had decided to make the most of their retirement by seeing how many stamps they could add

to their passports before they grew too old and
feeble to globetrot. They were part of the new generation of fashionable retirees. They'd visited the
Pyramids of Giza, the Great Wall of China and
were currently on an extended tour of Europe.

Rowan had one brother, who naturally be-
grudged their parents the fruit of their hard-earned
labor and, rather than admiring them for packing
as much *living* into their lives as she did, only be-
moaned the loss of his dwindling inheritance.
Though they both lived in Middleton, she rarely
saw him, which, sadly, was fine with her.

Were her parents aware of her circumstances,
Rowan knew they wouldn't hesitate to help her
out, but pride, the insistent desire to fend for herself and the idea that they might miss another
stamp because of her kept her from asking. She
scowled. Besides, her brother had his hand out
often enough for both of them.

She could make it on her own.

Would make it on her own. All she had to do
was get through another month, then hopefully
she'd get called back to school. Until then, she'd
just answer her 1-900 line every time it rang and
take care of her neighbor. It was a small price to
pay for her independence.

Rowan summoned a weak smile as Ida drew

near and silently—fervently—prayed that the woman hadn't developed another ingrown toenail.

"I swear, you're the dirtiest female I think I've ever seen," Ida chided. "Gardening is dirty work, I'll grant you. But—" her lips twisted with displeasure as she inventoried every smudge and smear on Rowan's body "—I think that you get down and roll in it." Her lined face folded into a frown. "How do you ever expect to find a man when you look more fit to be the bride of a pig?"

Rowan barely smothered a sigh. In addition to being part of the *no-eyebrow* generation, Ida was also of the outdated opinion that a woman wasn't complete until she had a man to make her whole. It was penis envy to the *nth* degree and the mentality never ceased to make her grind her teeth in frustration.

Furthermore, Rowan had been burned once and, call her crazy, but she simply wasn't up to a repeat performance of that disaster at the moment. She'd been in love, imagining the happily ever after that Ida relentlessly preached—she'd even reluctantly let that bastard drive her car, her biggest regret because he hadn't been *vintage-Vette worthy* and she'd known it—but hadn't heeded her own intuition because she'd been too busy picking out china patterns and bridesmaids' dresses. She'd tricked herself into thinking that she was in love, and he'd tricked her into believing he reciprocated the sentiment.

He'd been reciprocating something all right, but it hadn't been with her.

Two weeks before the wedding, she'd shown up at her fiancé's apartment for some surprise sex. It turned out to be surprise sex, too, only she was the one surprised and he was the one having sex.

Bitter pill, hard lesson.

Since then, she'd developed an unspoken code of sorts, one that her father had unwittingly inspired. She didn't date anyone who didn't fully appreciate her car, and she didn't sleep with anyone who had the gall to ask to drive it. Bizarre? Yes. But it worked.

Rowan glanced at the sleek little convertible parked in her driveway and felt her lips curl at the corners. Dubbed the first American sports car, the Vette was an unparalleled testament to fine engineering at its best. Honduras Maroon with fawn interior and a white ragtop, it had a 327 V-eight with four on the floor, and it purred with megahorsepower perfection. It had been her dad's first brandnew car and he'd cared for it with the kind of reverent regard the vehicle deserved. She'd shared his passion and, as a result, he'd handed her the keys when she'd graduated from high school.

Rowan had decided that while she might not be

a '62 Vette, she nonetheless deserved the same care and attention, and the same reverence. Until she found a guy willing to ante up all of the above, she planned to play her cards close to her vest. Did she occasionally long for more? Of course she did. She enjoyed her independence, yes, but not to the point of being a perpetual loner. There were nights when the silence closed in around her and she literally ached for the presence of another body. A big, warm masculine body. Nights when she craved conversation and companionship, a lover and friend. A safe harbor amid the ordered chaos of her life. But she refused to settle for anything less than the total package, and therein lay the rub.

Ignoring Ida's bride-of-a-pig remark, Rowan summoned a smile. "Was there something I could do for you, Ida?"

Ida started. Her preoccupied gaze darted away from Rowan's grimy shirt and settled on her face. Then she frowned, huffed an exaggerated breath and fished a napkin from the front pocket of her housecoat. "Honestly," Ida complained as she wiped Rowan's cheek. "It's all over your face, too." She tsked under her breath. "I hope you're hosing yourself down before you climb into that old tub. Those drains are slow enough as it is."

"I always do," Rowan lied easily. Ida was forever offering little tips on how to care for the aging guest house. *Don't overload the circuits. Use oil soap to clean the floors.* Ida Holcomb was a woman of many opinions and she could be counted on to share them—liberally—whether one wanted to hear them or not. A droll smiled curled Rowan's lips.

Seemingly satisfied, the older woman stuffed the napkin back into her pocket. "There. That's better, though I really wish you had time to change. You're my representative, you know," she said, drawing herself up primly. "How you look reflects directly upon me."

So an errand was in order, Rowan thought, resisting the urge to smile. "I can change in a flash, Ida. Where do you need me to go?"

"To the drug store." She winced uncomfortably and rubbed her belly. "The fiber and prunes didn't do the trick. I need an enema."

And she should definitely be turned out for that mission, Rowan thought dimly, equally horrified and revolted. After all, buying an enema was important business. But just par for the course in her train wreck of a life. She was so used to being humiliated she often wondered what it would feel like to be normal. To not blush or squirm or writhe with embarrassment.

Rowan swallowed, nodded jerkily, not trusting herself to speak.

"In fact, you'd better get two. Better safe than sorry," Ida prophesied grimly.

Rowan managed a sick smile. *Right.* And better this than hungry, she tried to tell herself.

The argument might have worked, too…if she hadn't just lost her appetite.

2

AT THIRTY-TWO and in perfect health, Will Foster found himself skating the edge of an anger-induced aneurysm, or at the very least, a massive stroke.

Doris Whitaker had screwed him again.

Not in the literal sense, of course—Will shuddered as her heavily made-up, wrinkled face flashed through his mind's eye—but figuratively, he might as well have painted a big bull's-eye on his ass.

The ass she was undoubtedly watching, the old perv, Will thought with an unhappy start as he strode across her yard to his truck. He cast a glance over his shoulder, and sure enough, she'd been watching him leave. Her painted lips slid into a wider smile and she twinkled her arthritic, bejeweled fingers at him.

Will forced a tight smile and waved back. "Goodbye," he muttered through gritted teeth.

His company, Foster's Landscape Design, had

spent the better part of three summers, not to mention thousands of dollars, trying to fulfill their "satisfaction guaranteed" promise.

To no avail.

Though he knew he should simply let it go—should simply concede defeat—perversely, Will couldn't do it. He'd get that satisfied-customer stamp of approval from her, dammit, or die trying. It was the point of it. All bragging aside, he was good at what he did. He *loved* his job. Loved developing a landscape, then pulling it together and seeing it to fruition. Loved getting his hands dirty, nursing blooms and watching things grow. He had a tremendous amount of respect for the codependent design of the world. The whole oxygen and carbon dioxide cycle that made plants and animals dependent on one another. It was…awe-inspiring.

Furthermore, Foster's Landscape Design was swiftly approaching their ten-year anniversary and in those ten years, he'd *never* had an unsatisfied customer.

He absolutely refused to let Doris ruin that record.

His team had finished up today and, though she'd been pleased throughout the process—had approved the design herself *once again*—she'd decided that it wasn't what she'd wanted after all.

Tear it out and start over.

Will had wanted to tear something out all right, but it hadn't been the cacti she'd decided she hated. This was the *third* freakin' time she'd pulled this shit. He was at his wit's end, and quite honestly, if he wasn't afraid she'd howl blue murder down at that country club she virtually funded, he'd be tempted to tell her to take that cactus and shove it up her—

Two loud beeps, followed by his mother screaming "Will?" into the two-way radio interrupted the uncharitable thought. Despite the fact that he'd told her repeatedly that yelling wasn't necessary, Millie Foster, perversely, continued to do it. On purpose, he suspected, because it never failed to startle the hell out of him.

Will swore, unsnapped the combination radio/phone from his belt and dredged the bottom of his soul for an ounce of unspent patience. He squeezed his eyes tightly shut. "Mother, for the last time, you *don't* have to yell."

"Sorry," Millie replied unrepentantly. "I just wanted to make sure that you heard me."

"I heard you. What's up?" Will detected a bit of laughter and catcalling in the background. He frowned. "What's going on?"

"I just wanted to let you know that you have a dinner date tonight, so be sure and finish up in time to take a proper bath."

Dinner date? Will thought, utterly confused. A

proper bath? He hadn't made a date with anyone. In fact, he hadn't had a date in months. Even if he'd met someone who'd sparked any interest—which he hadn't—he wouldn't have had the time. Spring was the busiest season of his year, the time of year when his laughable social life was shoved to the back burner. Besides, his last serious relationship had left a bad taste in his mouth—a combination of bitter regret, bad judgment and plain stupidity—and it wasn't a flavor he wished to sample again anytime soon.

Will frowned as the implication of this conversation finally surfaced in his muddled brain and he mentally swore—she was matchmaking.

Again.

His grim mood blackened further. Though he loved her to distraction, and he knew she simply had his best interests at heart, Will nonetheless was exceedingly weary of her meddling. "Mother, I didn't make a date for tonight, and if you have made one for me, then you'll be the one to cancel it. We've been down this road, and I'm not in the mood to backtrack. Not today."

An exasperated huff sounded. "Don't you want to know who it's with before I cancel it?"

He wasn't remotely curious. "No," he said flatly.

"Fine," his mother replied. "Ordinarily I wouldn't have seen the need to meddle—"

Ha! Will thought.

"But," she sighed, and a curious, almost ominous quiver had entered her voice. "I just thought that, given this ph—phone bill, that desperate m-measures should be t-taken."

More guffaws, more laughter from her end, and he could have sworn he heard his brother, Ben, say, "Hell, yeah! An inflatable woman would have been cheaper." But that couldn't possibly be right, Will thought, thoroughly confused, because it didn't make any sense. And his phone bill? What was wrong with his phone bill, and what did that have to do with her finding him a date?

Will developed an eye twitch. He shoved the key in the ignition and started the truck. "Make sense, Mom. What are you talking about? What's wrong with my phone bill?"

"Nothing…if you don't mind that it's five times more than last month."

"What?" But that would make it—Will did the mental calculation and blinked, astounded—right at a thousand dollars. His jaw all but dropped.

"You sound surprised, dear," she continued blithely. "I guess you didn't realize how long you spent t-talking to y-your 1-900-Lover." She dissolved into a fit of whooping, wheezing laughter that made his face burn. "At any rate, a real date would have been cheaper, which is why I can't in good conscience call Rebecca Hillendale and cancel on your behalf. There are times when a mother simply must intervene."

For the first time in his life, Will Foster knew what it felt like to be literally struck dumb. Not dumb as in he couldn't speak, but dumb as in *stupid,* as in he had a brain, but couldn't for the life of him make it function. Several thoughts swirled simultaneously through his head, but they were disjointed and dim, and he lacked the cognitive ability to put them in any sort of order, much less get them out of his mouth.

The best he could figure out, somehow—and God only knew how—1-900-charges, presumably for *phone sex*—had ended up on his phone bill. Apparently—and much to his immediate, unwarranted humiliation—his mother had broadcast this at the office—where she'd seemingly forgotten that she worked *for him*—and then had taken it upon herself to find him a date.

Meanwhile, Rebecca Hillendale was a humpbacked harpy with the disposition of a constipated porcupine and he'd rather die a slow painful death or have his testicles removed with red-hot pincers than to sit through a meal with her. These were the thoughts roiling through his tortured mind, but when he finally managed to speak, it was in short staccato sentences devoid of any emotion except outrage.

"Mother, I'll be there in a minute." Will slipped the transmission into reverse, backed into the street, then dropped the gear shift into drive. The truck shot forward. "Nobody leaves."

"But—"

"*Nobody leaves.*"

AN HOUR LATER Will's mind was in order, but his temper was not.

According to the phone company, the calls Will insisted that he hadn't made, had, in fact, been dialed from his number. Curiously, during hours that he was at work. Another look at the bill—at the dates the calls were placed, specifically—had shed a new light on the situation.

The calls had coincided with his nephew's visit.

Scott, his sister's eldest son, typically spent every spring break with Will. Usually Will put him to work, but a four-wheeler accident the week before Scott's visit had foiled that plan. Scott had been forced to spend the holiday playing catch-up on his studies, and Will had decided it would be shitty to cancel the kid's visit simply because he'd lose the labor.

Given the make-up work situation, he'd had to plead with his sister for the ungrateful brat to even come, and now as thanks, Scott had put him in a horrible position—he'd left him with a whopping *thousand dollar* phone bill and the unhappy task of telling his sister that her child had been having phone sex on Will's watch.

Which led him to his present errand.

Before he called his sister and shared that little tidbit—before he paid the bill, even—he intended to directly contact the author of his misery—the phone sex operator. Over the top? Probably. But what the hell—his normally sedate life had been knocked off-kilter today and he had to do something proactive to put it back on the right path. He couldn't help it. It was all part and parcel of being a professed control freak. Will took exception to the unflattering term, but couldn't deny his nature. He liked to do things *his way,* liked having *his way,* and ninety-nine-point-nine percent of the time he could say with confidence that *his way* was the *right way.*

Will's first impulse had been to call the 1-900 line, but he'd quickly changed his mind. The unscrupulous witch wasn't bleeding another friggin' nickel out of him. Instead, he'd called a P.I. buddy to do a little snooping for him. The best Will had hoped for was a toll-free line, but what his friend had found had been considerably better. A name and address, and, wonder of wonders, a local one at that. What were the odds?

He'd been destined to blast her.

Given the morning from hell he'd had, to be honest, Will didn't think he'd ever looked forward to doing anything more.

When he'd learned that the woman lived here it was as though Christmas had come early. Rather than taking out his miserable mood on Doris—who he resignedly admitted he would be forced to continue to work with—or his well-meaning but meddlesome mother—whom he'd live to regret pissing off—Will had found out that he could verbally assault a perfect stranger who really deserved it, and finally blow off the steam which had been steadily building since early this morning.

What better person to verbally eviscerate than a woman so lacking in morals that she'd have phone sex with a teenager? A minor? A mere child?

Granted, Scott was seventeen and, given the way the girls followed him around, the kid was most likely getting laid more frequently and with more furor than his uncle. Will nevertheless thought the woman should have used better judgment. But she hadn't. She'd crossed the line in order to pad her own pockets—with *his* money, dammit—and for that, she would pay.

A Jackson native, Will had been at once familiar and surprised by the supposed address of the woman. According to his buddy, she lived in an old but affluent neighborhood on a street one wouldn't normally expect to find an unsavory phone sex operator in residence.

Wisteria Court was located in the historical district. Huge antebellum homes reminiscent of a bygone era, with aged boxwoods, magnolias, weeping willows and tulip trees stood sentinel on the manicured lawns. The neighborhood was rife with the scent of mint juleps and old money, and he found the idea of a phone sex operator in residence among Jackson's so-called hoity-toity set perversely funny. Ordinarily, the idea would have drawn a smile.

But not today. Today, he was too pissed.

He slowed the truck to a crawl as he checked house numbers, then finally hitting pay dirt, he wheeled the vehicle into the appropriate drive. Anticipation spiked. *Finally,* Will thought. He purposely stoked his ire on the way to the door by alternately imagining writing the check to the phone company, and telling his sister about Scott's foray into the seedy world of phone sex—*Reach out and touch someone,* indeed, Will thought darkly. So, by the time he plied the knocker every last particle of irritation he'd had that morning set ready on his tongue. He'd pulled back the hammer, so to speak, and was ready to unload.

It was to his vast disappointment then, when an elderly woman with pink foam curlers in her hair answered the door and he was forced to put on the safety.

Again.

He stifled the burgeoning urge to scream.

"Can I help you?" she asked.

Baffled, Will frowned. He knew he had the right address. But this... He inwardly shuddered. This couldn't possibly be the right woman. "Er...Ms. Crosswhite?"

"Nope. Ida Holcomb. You're looking for Rowan," she said matter-of-factly. She jerked a thumb over her shoulder. "She lives in the guest house in the back." The woman gasped, laid a hand over her belly, and shot him a pained look. "Gotta go," she said abruptly, then slammed the door in his face.

Startled, Will drew back, then, shaking his head, made his way off the porch and toward the rear of the property where the older woman had indicated. He had a bead on her now, Will thought, purposefully striding alongside the house. As he rounded the corner, however, the sight that greeted him caused him to slow and every bit of the anger he'd nursed faded into insignificance.

A vintage Vette—a '62 if he wasn't mistaken— in pristine condition sat in the drive next to the house. He whistled low and, had his attention not been instantly drawn elsewhere, he would have been tempted to inspect the car from bumper to bumper. As it was, his gaze had landed on the house and surrounding property, and any notion of the car, while it was admittedly a fine piece of machinery, drifted right out of his head.

The house, a miniature version of the primary residence sat at the very back of the property. White frame, double verandah, utterly charming. But it hadn't been what made him pause, either— it was the garden around the house that had made such an impact. He blinked, pulling it all into focus, and for some wholly unknown reason, an excited tingle started in the heels of his feet and swiftly moved upward.

Will had been in landscape design for years, had been to countless shows in practically every part of the country, and yet nothing in his experience could compare to *this*.

Though he recognized every flower, vine, shrub and bush—all of them typical to the average bee-and-butterfly garden—the whimsical layout, the use of color and texture combined with what he could only deduce was the owner's original metalwork and stained glass made it the most *unique* garden he'd ever seen. There was no discernable plan, no clear-cut layout, and yet everything grew together in a seamless form of ordered pandemonium.

It was *gorgeous*.

Butterfly bushes, creeping flox, flowering peach and crabapple trees, clematis vines, various lilies, and bedding plants, a variety of ground covers, and perhaps the most interesting of all—antique roses. The swamp rose, in particular, was one that he coveted.

Feeling like he'd been clubbed over the head again, Will slowly resumed his pace. Inexplicably drawn to the roses, the grand dames of antique bushes, he reverently fingered one delicate petal while quietly inspecting the plant. No spots or aphids, and what minimal pruning had been done had been accomplished with a precisely loving hand. Whoever tended this garden had a passion for the process and clearly designed it for their own personal enjoyment.

Not a single detail had been left untended and, despite the fact that he knew this was the work of the skanky phone sex operator, of all people, Will found himself grudgingly impressed. More than impressed. Floored, really. After all, it took a helluva lot of imagination, not to mention a great deal of time and effort to—

The tinkle of feminine laughter drifted to him, snagging his attention back to the task at hand. He scanned the yard and, after a moment, his gaze landed upon a generously rounded, denim-clad rump peeking out from a small raised bed in the far corner of the garden. A pair of tanned, equally shapely legs were attached to the rump. He could see little else save the back of her head, and while he got the impression of long sable-colored hair, in all truthfulness as far as he was concerned she could have been bald and he'd never have noticed—he was too busy admiring her ass.

And oh, what an ass it was.

Full, curvy and heart-shaped, it gently tested the strength of the seams of her roomy cutoffs and accentuated what he could tell even from this distance was a small waist.

She flicked a weed off to her side where a growing pile accumulated on the lawn. "Oh, you naughty boy," she said, her voice the perfect mixture of flirtatious and intimate. She laughed again, a long wanton giggle that too effectively conjured images of twisted sheets and bare limbs, made the fine hairs on his arms stand on end and a hum of attraction vibrate his spine.

Who the hell was she talking to? Will wondered, trying to peer around her. He frowned, intrigued. Who was a naughty boy? He didn't see any boy. She leaned back on her haunches, seemingly admiring her handiwork and he saw it then— the headset. In a moment of blind, dawning comprehension he realized what she was doing.

Or *having,* rather—phone sex.

Right here in her yard. While weeding her garden.
It literally blew what was left of his mind.

"Oh, Roy," she sighed convincingly. "I'm hot, too. Maybe I should get undressed, slip out of this teddy. There's not much to it, but I like being naked. It makes me feel…wicked. Would you like that, Roy?"

Apparently *Roy* did like the idea, Will thought with a wry twist of his lips, because she chuckled softly again. To his astonishment, he felt that sound hiss through his own blood. Felt a curious sense of excitement—one that was almost foreign to him since it had been so long—fizz through his abdomen.

"Okay, I'm ready," she murmured. "What do you want to do to me first?" Another wanton chuckle, then, "You're right. Foreplay *is* highly overrated. And there's no need, because I'm ready for you right now."

What happened next, Will would have never believed if he hadn't seen—and heard—it with his own eyes and ears.

The woman cooed, winced, groaned and moaned into the phone as though Roy weren't God-knows-where, but instead rooted right there between her delectable thighs. Her breath came in short little puffs—while she enthusiastically attacked the weeds, no less—and she threw in the occasional *"Oh, God! Oh, please! Oh, yes, Roy,*

God yes!" and then rounded out her performance with the most convincing sounding orgasm he'd ever heard.

When her breathing finally slowed, Will felt like he'd been through the wringer. Impossibly, his heart rate had jumped into overdrive, every milligram of moisture had evaporated from his mouth and he'd come within a hairsbreadth of an immaculate orgasm himself, a phenomenon that hadn't happened to him since he'd first hit puberty. At some point, he'd reached down and held on to her fence, undoubtedly to remain upright because his knees had grown decidedly weak.

"Oh, I enjoyed it, too, Roy," she murmured, her voice laced with feigned pleasant exhaustion. "You're the best," she told him, blatantly catering to the man's ego. "Call me again sometime, okay?"

To his continued astonishment, she blithely ended the call and went back to weeding, as though nothing remarkable had happened.

Slack-jawed, Will could only stare at her. He blinked. Then blinked again. Though he'd come here with the intention of blasting her into oblivion, curiously his anger had been replaced with a combination of brooding fascination, compelling intrigue and an unwanted smidge of reluctant admiration.

He'd also found the whole thing hilariously funny.

He smothered a chuckle, lifted his hands and began to clap.

His prey gasped, then turned and bright green—*true green*—eyes tangled with his.

Will almost staggered from the impact. The bottom dropped out of his stomach and, though he knew it was impossible, he felt the ground quake beneath his feet. An electric current zinged up his spine, then back-tracked and settled hotly behind his zipper.

With effort, Will managed to recover. "Very good, Ms. Crosswhite." He summoned a weak chuckle. "I don't think I've ever seen anyone enjoy…w-weeding quite as m-much as you."

3

ROWAN WAS ACCUSTOMED to being humiliated. Frankly, she'd long ago resigned herself to the fact that she would stay in a chronic state of humiliation. The level would simply vary, but being humiliated, she knew, was a foregone conclusion.

For instance, buying the enemas today had been humiliating—almost as humiliating as the time she'd had to buy Ida's wart remover.

Or the time she'd inadvertently pulled a tampon out of her purse and tried to write a check with it.

Or the time she'd accidentally crammed a straw up her nose and caused it to bleed.

Or the time she'd shut her *own ear* in the car door.

She was constantly getting herself into situations that made her want to shrink out of existence, or at the very least out of someone's immediate memory. She routinely fell, got choked…*something* all the time. Humiliating? Yes, every last event.

But nothing—*nothing*—in her past or present

memory could compare to the absolute mortification of this moment.

She wanted to die.

Truly, desperately wanted to die.

Because the hunk leaning against her fence had apparently heard every last syllable of her most recent conversation, from the first *Oh, God* to the final *Oooohhhh,* and every dramatic pant, wince and groan in between.

Heat scalded her cheeks, and if she hadn't already turned around to face him, she would have pretended to be deaf, maybe even blind. Anything to avoid this panic-stricken *oh-shit-not-again* scenario. Rowan tried consoling herself with the old whatever-doesn't-kill-you-will-make-you-stronger adage—her normal pep-me-up cheer—but for whatever reason, the message fell flat this time.

Though it took every iota of willpower she possessed and because she was the mistress of her world, Rowan stood, dusted her hands off and reluctantly began to make her way across the yard. And the closer she got, the more humiliated she became. Her heart sank and she swallowed a whimper.

Naturally, he had to be gorgeous.

The guy had been a hunk from a distance—casually messy blond hair, a great smile, broad shoulders and nice legs. But up close, he was downright devastating. His hair was sun-bleached, a dark tawny color around his ears and nape, but several shades lighter on top. His face was lean and tanned, with a mouth slightly fuller than average and a pair of light brown eyes that offset the alpha bone structure with just a hint of boy-next-door. It was a face that said, "Best friend or worst enemy? You choose," and the compelling combination made a shiver dance up her spine.

"Can I help you?" Rowan finally managed.

"I'm Will Foster," the guy told her. His smile faded and, unfortunately, a less pleasant look claimed his intriguing features.

So, worst enemy, was it? Rowan thought. Interesting.

"I'm here because your number showed up on my phone bill this month," he continued, his otherwise nice voice throbbing with barely suppressed outrage. He crossed his arms over his well-muscled chest and an irritating smirk ruined the look of that gorgeous mouth. "But *I* didn't call you."

"If that's the case, then you'll need to contact the phone company," Rowan replied, automatically offering the most expedient solution to his problem. Her nature, she couldn't help it. She could plant a whimsical garden, draw, paint and create different types of funky art, but put a problem in front of her and she'd find the most efficient answer. She was an anomaly, a right-brained thinker with left-brained tendencies.

The left brain kicked in when she belatedly realized that he shouldn't even be here. How had he gotten her address? Her name? A finger of unease prodded her spine. "How did you get my address, Mr.—"

"Foster," he reminded her tightly. "And I did contact the phone company. They told me your number had been dialed from my house, which meant the *thousand-dollar* charges were correct."

Rowan scowled, baffled. "If the charges were correct, then what are you doing here?"

This was over the line, she thought, instinctively backing away from him. If there'd been a problem that the phone company couldn't resolve, then why hadn't he simply called? Why had he gone to the trouble to track her down? Common sense told her she should be alarmed, but the intense irritation stiffening every muscle in her body negated the logical emotion. Her eyes narrowed. *Of all the damned nerve...*

"I'm here because you had phone sex with my nephew," he retorted angrily. "My *underage* nephew."

Rowan's first impulse was to deny the charge—she knew perfectly well that she hadn't had phone sex with a minor...but she had talked to one.

The flash of insight jimmied an exasperated grunt from her throat and she managed a slight smile. "You're Scott's uncle, aren't you?" She'd been expecting this. Not *this* as in a visit, but at least that explained why he'd gone to the trouble to find her. She relaxed marginally. Things were beginning to make sense.

His lips twisted into another annoying smirk. "I'm impressed, Ms. Crosswhite. For a thousand dollars you should remember his name."

The smart-ass was making it damned hard to forget her self-righteous anger, Rowan thought, heartily annoyed. Pity she couldn't forget how gorgeous he was. "I remember his name because he called me several times."

"I know." He fished what she recognized as his phone bill from the back pocket of his shorts and ran an eye over it. She watched in a sort of drunken fascination as his lips moved, counting off the calls. "Six times, to be precise."

Rowan pushed her hair over her shoulder and assumed a negligent pose, struggled to detach her gaze from those distracting lips. "That sounds about right."

"Did you realize that he was underage? Or did you just not care?"

Rowan knew that he had every reason to be upset, particularly since he was laboring under the mistaken assumption that she'd had phone sex with his nephew. Nevertheless, she didn't appreciate the sarcasm or the censure, and she sure as hell didn't appreciate being tracked down at her house, having her privacy violated.

"Yes, I knew he was underage—"

His lips curled without humor and he rocked back on his heels. "Then you just didn't care. But you will care, Ms. Crosswhite, when his parents prosecute you."

Rowan felt her eyes widen. "You're probably right. However, being as I've done nothing to be prosecuted for, then I don't have anything to worry about, do I?"

"Phone sex with a minor—"

Her patience snapped and she barely stifled the urge to scream. "I didn't have phone sex with your nephew, Mr. Foster," Rowan all but growled. "I helped him with his science homework."

For a split second his face went comically blank, then a smug disbelieving smile drifted over his too-gorgeous lips. "And what were you doing with *Roy,* I wonder?" he drawled lazily. "Teaching him the difference between a consonant and a vowel?"

Renewed embarrassment flooded her cheeks and while she had appreciated the fact that he owned a sense of humor, she didn't appreciate it being at her expense. Rowan pulled in a deep calming breath and called upon her past experience with irate parents to see her through this provoking scene. She'd dealt with enough of them over the years to handle this, she told herself. One of them had to remain professional, and clearly it wasn't *him*.

"Have you spoken to Scott?" she asked, striving for a calm she didn't feel. "Have you asked him what happened?"

"No, I haven't." A muscle jumped in his tense jaw. "Since I'll have to tell his mother first, it's not a conversation that I'm looking forward to."

"Well, you can handle that however you want to," she retorted, "but as for my part, I have proof that I didn't have phone sex with Scott, Mr. Foster." And she did, thank God, Rowan thought, immensely relieved.

A perplexed line emerged between his brows. "Proof?"

"I have a record feature on my phone. For safety reasons," she clarified at his astounded look. Honestly. "Kooks, weirdoes, harassment—"

Comprehension dawned and he nodded abruptly.

"Anyway, when I realized that Scott was underage—which was almost immediately—I hit record." She pulled a shrug. "In fact, I've recorded every conversation with Scott and will have to insist that you listen to them, just so there's no misunderstanding. I thought I might hear from an outraged parent—or an uncle, as it's turned out—though, frankly, I thought that I'd receive a phone call." She pinned him with a weighty stare. "Which brings me back to my first question—how did you get my name and address?" she persisted. "How did you find me? Because to be quite honest with you, Mr. Foster, it, uh… It kind of freaks me out."

And it did. Anonymity had been her first line of defense. Only one other person knew about her side-job—her best friend, Alexa, and Rowan knew beyond a shadow of a doubt that Alexa hadn't betrayed her confidence. Her friend was one of those rare souls who could actually keep a secret.

But if this guy found her this easily, who was to say that another guy couldn't? One without an understandable cause? It completely unnerved her. In this case, Rowan could easily see what had happened. His nephew had made the calls and, in addition to paying for them, he'd have to tell the kid's parents. She grimaced. Not fun, she'd agree. Nevertheless…

For the first time he seemed to consider that he'd made a mistake, a tactical error of sorts and he knew it. He shifted uneasily, rubbed a hand over the back of his neck, and shot her an uncomfortable look. "I, uh… I have a friend in the P.I. business," he reluctantly admitted. "He made a few calls."

She cocked her head and shrewdly considered him. "I see. I'm assuming since this friend was able to give you my name and address, he also had my regular telephone number." She paused, and was rewarded when he started to squirm. "And yet you still decided that a visit was in order."

He winced, looked out over her garden, then shot her a sheepish smile. That half grin had to be one of the sexiest things she'd ever seen and it had the singular ability to drain every bit of the irritation still inhabiting her spine. "I was pissed."

Oh, she'd just bet he was, Rowan thought, resisting the urge to smile herself. "Well, since you're here, you should probably listen to those tapes."

He started. "Right."

Without waiting to see if he followed her, Rowan turned and headed toward the house. For some unknown reason, her stomach did a little anticipation-overload flop, and the back of her nape prickled with awareness. An indication of just how pathetic she was, she decided with an inward harrumph of disgust.

Jesus.

This guy hadn't tracked her down to follow through with an initial attraction—he'd come over here with the express purpose of chewing her up and spitting her out. He'd bared his big-bad-wolf teeth and had planned to make a meal out of her. One, by the looks of things, he'd fully intended to enjoy.

Rowan darted a look over her shoulder and felt a perverse flame of heat lick her belly. She smiled and bit her lip.

Pity she wasn't ready to be served up on a platter…yet.

4

WILL'S GAZE inexplicably dropped to Rowan's retreating ass. Then the retreating part triggered in his sluggish brain, and it belatedly occurred to him that he was supposed to be following her. Annoyed, he cursed under his breath and hurried after her.

She paused on the front porch, giving him time to catch up. She wore a faint smile, as though she knew precisely why the minimal wait had been necessary.

To his absolute astonishment, he felt a blush creep into his cheeks.

The phone sex operator was making *him* blush.

How screwed up was that?

Hell, he didn't know why he expected anything to be normal today, of all days, when this had been the most bizarre few hours of his life, most specifically the past few minutes.

Only seconds ago, he'd listened to this woman fake an orgasm over the phone, then rather than having the decency to be the stereotypical bored, homely housewife, she had the nerve to be gorgeous. Not passably pretty, or merely nice to look at.

She was gorgeous.

She was hometown-beauty-queen-meets-wet-dream-porn-star and, despite all reason, he found himself absolutely intrigued by her. Hell, who was he trying to kid? He'd been intrigued by her from the first sultry syllable he'd heard her utter to dear old Roy.

Then, before he'd thought better of it, he'd applauded her performance, and she'd turned around…and he'd gone from being slightly curious to downright captivated.

His impression of her hair had been right. It was long and dark brown, and it slithered over her shoulders, cascaded down her back and landed in a gentle wave a couple of inches below her waist. It was sexy as hell and, while it was politically incorrect, it evoked the caveman in him—not to mention several other primal urges he'd had to forcibly tamp down.

She had a kind, open face with high cheekbones, a pair of bright green eyes that glinted with equal amounts of humor and intelligence, and a ripe mouth the color of a dusky pink rose. And the voice that came out of that mouth…

Mercy.

Sweet and slightly husky, almost sleepy, for a

lack of better description. She could undoubtedly read the possible side effects on a medical-warning label and make it sound sexy.

In addition—as though those things weren't enough—she drove a vintage Vette, was obviously a master gardener as well as an artisan and, though she possessed a healthy modest streak—she'd blushed to the roots of her hair when he'd caught her verbally servicing Roy, he thought wryly—she'd chosen phone sex, of all things, as her career path.

The combined incongruity was astounding.

She was the proverbial riddle wrapped in an enigma...and there was nothing more interesting to Will than the challenge of a good mystery.

He let his gaze drift slowly over her as he followed her inside the house and mentally rocked back on his heels. Figuring her out would undoubtedly be a treat—one he'd most likely forfeited the minute he'd flown off the handle and violated her privacy, he reminded himself grimly. Sheesh. What the hell had he been thinking? Will wondered. Had he lost his freakin' mind? What on earth had possessed him to track her down—

She threw him a look over her shoulder, and he caught a glimpse of continued humor in those leaf-green eyes. "Let me wash my hands, then I'll get those tapes."

Oh, yeah. The tapes. Will frowned. Considering

he'd made a grand show of running her to ground, he figured he'd better look interested in listening to them. He arranged his face into what he hoped look like a serious, slightly perturbed expression and, rather than continuing to study her—a perpetual impulse—he let his gaze roam around her house.

Like its owner, it created an instant impression.

It boasted beautiful hardwood floors, tall floor-to-ceiling windows and lots of heavily carved molding and trim work which was a prevalent theme in the traditional antebellum style.

But the similarities to traditional ended there.

Fresh-cut flowers in old light-blue Mason jars lined the mantel. Stained glass dressed every window, and hand-painted furniture and art—obviously hers—rounded out the eclectic decor. Lots of color, energy and light. The whimsical design reminded him of her garden—it was distinctly unique.

Like her.

"Okay," the object of his instant fascination said as she breezed back into the room. "I've got them."

Once again, Will feigned appropriate concern, but from the sidelong glance she slid him combined with the slight quiver of her full lips, he didn't think he'd successfully maintained the ruse.

Hell, he didn't doubt for a moment that the whole damned scenario was precisely as she'd claimed. She wouldn't have offered proof otherwise, and though he'd been initially horrified that she recorded her conversations—his distrustful mind had immediately leaped to some form of blackmail—he had to grudgingly admit that it was quite a crafty move. Smart, really.

An antique display case which housed mismatched china pieces and other bric-a-brac served as a counter of sorts. Butted against the lower kitchen cabinets, the old piece formed a bar between the kitchen and living room.

Rowan shifted a few items aside and hefted a boom box, along with a couple other tapes onto the glass surface. While she wrestled with the plug, the things she'd moved out of the way snagged his attention. His eyes widened and, before he could check the impulse, a startled laugh, which he barely morphed into a cough, broke up in his throat.

A bottle of strawberry wine, three enemas and two treatments of wart remover stood on the makeshift counter.

Rowan started, then shot him a look and ultimately followed his gaze. She inhaled sharply, then closed her eyes tightly shut and groaned miserably. Color bloomed on her cheeks and she sank her teeth into that ripe bottom lip. "The wine is mine," she said haltingly, obviously—adorably—mortified. "The other things…are not."

"That's a relief." Will felt his lips twitch. He crossed his arms over his chest and lifted one shoulder in a negligent shrug. "For a moment there I was afraid you were a warty, constipated alcoholic."

The comment drew a droll smile and, while he couldn't be sure, he thought he saw a flash of reciprocated interest in those too-perceptive green eyes.

"I'm the alcoholic," she deadpanned. "My landlord is warty and constipated."

He grimaced, shifted and rubbed a hand over the back of his neck. "That's...unfortunate," Will finally managed, unable to come up with anything that remotely resembled an appropriate response.

"Ah," she sighed knowingly. A ghost of a smile played on her lips and she crossed her arms over her chest, then leaned a curvy hip against the counter. "So you *can* be tactful." She paused, allowing the dart to penetrate, then continued before he could respond. "I run errands for her," she explained. "As you can imagine, buying those particular items—" she glanced meaningfully at the ignoble remedies "—results in considerable embarrassment. So," she sighed wistfully, "in the vain hope that I could preserve a little dignity, I decided to stockpile them." Eyes twinkling, her gaze darted to him and she blew out a resigned breath. "Clearly, it didn't work."

For whatever reason, Will got the distinct impression that her efforts to thwart humiliation rarely worked. He smiled, unreasonably enchanted. "Ah, well. Better luck next time," he offered, once again unable to conjure an artful remark.

She chuckled grimly, pulled a slight shrug, then turned her attention back to the tapes. "One can hope." She slipped a tape into the player, and hit the rewind button. "So Scott's your nephew? How old is he? Sixteen? Seventeen?"

"Seventeen."

"He seems like a good kid. Bright."

"He is. Though obviously his judgment isn't always on the mark," he added pointedly.

Rather than being insulted, she merely smiled. "He's a teenager," she said, as though that explained everything. "They're a breed apart until those hormones level out. Particularly boys."

Interestingly, her matter-of-fact tone resonated with the voice of experience. Still… Will grimaced. "I don't think that excuse is going to fly with his mother."

She depressed the play button and shot him an enigmatic look. "Then perhaps you should talk to his father."

Impressed with the insight, Will inclined his head. Actually, he'd considered bypassing his sister and talking to Jim. Jim, he knew, would at least understand the motivation behind his son's ignorant, thoughtless episode. He winced.

Lori…wouldn't.

She'd be angry and appalled, and the combination of the two wouldn't leave any room for understanding. Will had initially rejected the idea of bypassing Lori—it was the easy way out for him, ergo it had to be wrong. Now he wasn't so sure. Now he—

His thoughts ground to a halt as Rowan's voice, then his nephew's sounded from the machine—her sultry "Hello," then Scott's nervous squeak.

"Hi. I, uh…" He cleared his throat and his voice lowered to a comical level. "Hey. What's happening, baby?"

Will felt a smile tug at his lips and his gaze instinctively found hers. She, too, wore an amused expression.

"Look, Slick, you're not old enough to have this conversation," Rowan told him, instantly seeing through the ploy. "Call back in a few years."

"Wait!"

From there, things happened exactly the way she'd told him. They'd chatted, she'd tried to disconnect, citing the enormous phone bill someone would not approve of, and his nephew, to Will's astonishment, had glibly announced that his uncle wouldn't notice another 1-900 number because he frequently called them himself. In fact, Scott had continued, his uncle had probably called her in the past. Rowan had laughed at Will's outraged expression as he fervently denied the charge.

"I don't *need* to have phone sex," Will felt obliged to repeat after she'd turned off the tape. The unspoken *because-I-can-get-laid-without-it* hung between them, eliciting another mysterious smile from her. Her eyes twinkled.

"I'm sure you don't."

He nodded succinctly. "Damn straight."

She chewed the corner of her lip, presumably to keep from chuckling at his expense, and busied herself by putting the cassette away. She was laughing at him, Will knew, and he couldn't blame her because he was making a macho ass of himself. But he couldn't help it. It was a matter of honor, dammit. Men who could get laid in the traditional sense didn't call total strangers and whack off to the tune of a few well-rehearsed pants and sighs.

Phone sex? Will thought dubiously. Come on? He preferred his sexual encounters of the physical kind, thank you very much. He liked slow and tender, hot and frantic, and wasn't averse to a little kinky now and then. Sex was sex and, regardless of the method employed, hell, he thought with a slow smile, it was always good.

He'd never once thought about having a woman talk him through it...but he wasn't averse to a helping hand every now and then.

His gaze instantly drifted to her hands, and it took very little effort to imagine one of hers wrapped around him, touching him the way she'd implied she'd touched good ole Roy. A flash of heat detonated in his loins and a serious sense of excitement, one he hadn't felt in eons, pulsed through him.

She tucked her hair behind her ear. "Do you— Do you want to listen to the other tapes, or will that one suffice?"

Will grunted, unnerved. "That one will suffice."

She nodded, apparently still not trusting herself to look at him. "Good. Could I see that phone bill?"

He frowned, baffled. He couldn't imagine why, but he handed it to her nonetheless. "Sure."

Her lips moved as she silently scanned the bill, and it belatedly occurred to Will that she was tallying the multiple charges. In her head, without the aid of a calculator. Impressed, he readied his mouth to comment, but was interrupted as she handed the statement back to him. "Okay. Let me get my purse and I'll write you a check."

He blinked. "A check?"

"For the charges," she called over her shoulder. She disappeared into the back of the house, then emerged seconds later with a wallet. By the time she'd made the return trip, he'd managed to organize his chaotic thoughts into some semblance of order.

"Look, this isn't necessary. I didn't come here to get you to refund the charges." And he hadn't. Quite frankly, he hadn't thought beyond blasting her into oblivion, but he hardly needed to share that with her, did he?

She finished writing the check, scrawled her name across the bottom, then tore it out of the book and handed it to him. A smile caught the corner of her ripe mouth. "No, you came here to rip me a new one."

He'd opened his mouth to argue, but a guilty laugh emerged, beating him to the punch. He pulled a shrug. "Like I said, I was pissed."

"You don't say?" She batted her lashes with feigned innocence. "I hadn't noticed."

He owed her an apology, Will knew, and though saying he was sorry wasn't a phrase that came naturally to him—quite frankly, he wasn't used to being wrong—tendering the expected nicety now didn't seem quite so onerous.

He exhaled mightily. "Look, I'm sorry," he said, albeit awkwardly. He glanced at the floor and was momentarily distracted by her bare feet. Lots of toe rings and a small tattoo of a butterfly decorated the skin right above her pinkie toe. Another bolt of heat landed in his groin and he struggled to find the rest of the apology. "I— I shouldn't have come here. I, uh— I should have called."

"Yes, you should have," she replied levelly. "However, when Scott needed further tutoring, I should have given him my home number instead of continuing to let him call the 900-number." Her lips formed another droll smile, and her eyes twinkled with humor. "In my defense, I was trying to guard my privacy." She sighed softly. "At any rate, I intend to refund the charges, so just take the check, we'll be square and we can forget about this mess."

He doubted it, but he reluctantly pocketed the cash anyway. "At least let me pay you for the tutoring sessions," he offered. He laughed grimly. "Believe me, if the kid had asked me for help with science he would have been sadly disappointed."

If memory served, he'd barely passed science. Not because he'd lacked the intelligence or ability, he'd merely lacked the drive. Will had been one of those kids who survived high school by way of sports.

And—thanks to the kind hand of his father and grandfather—he'd known from the time he was old enough to plant a seed what he'd be doing with his life, so the only classes he'd been interested in throughout high school had been the ones that had pertained to agriculture.

Both his father and his grandfather had been farmers, had earned their living from the land. Corn, cotton, soy beans. Feast or famine, depending on the weather. They'd expected him to take the same route, but while Will had shared the same enthusiasm for the land, the same fascination with the soil and all she grew—the sheer interdependency of everything—he'd ultimately decided to carve his own path. He'd liked the combination of design, the challenge of outdoor architecture found in landscaping. He'd ridden through college on a football scholarship, had majored in landscape architecture with a minor in business administration, and the rest had been history. Unable to completely abandon his farming heritage, Will had added an heirloom seed catalog to his repertoire.

"No, those tutoring session are on me," Rowan told him, dragging him back into the conversation. She rolled her eyes. "Hell, I needed them as much as he did."

An important insight lurked behind that statement, Will decided. Intrigued, he arched a brow. "Oh?"

From her oh-hell expression, it was obvious that she thought she'd said too much. She swore under her breath, then released a pent-up sigh. "Oh, well," she finally relented. "It's not like you don't know everything else about me." She shot him a wry look. "I'm a teacher. I teach—" She winced grimly. "Correction, I *taught* science at Middleton High. Budget cuts ate my job, so until the system finds the money to put me back to work—hopefully in the fall—then I'm out of a contract." She shrugged, then bit her lip and, though she met his gaze directly, he detected a hint of vulnerability he instinctively knew that she'd resent. Which, curiously, made her all the more attractive. "For obvious reasons, I would appreciate your discretion. I, uh... I don't think the board of education would approve of my interim job."

Will mentally whistled. She'd certainly mastered the understatement. They wouldn't merely disapprove—they'd freak. A phone sex operator teaching their impressionable youth? Not here, not in this century.

The gravity of the situation he'd put her in finally dawned and he inwardly winced with regret. He'd royally screwed up by coming here. He'd literally jeopardized her livelihood. "Don't worry," he assured her. "Your secret's safe with me."

Her slim shoulders sank in obvious relief. "Thanks. I appreciate it."

"Can I ask you a question?"

She nodded. "Sure. Go ahead."

Will hesitated. "Why phone sex?" he finally blurted out. The question had been burning a hole in his brain. She was obviously smart, educated. Geez, God. Why phone sex, of all things? Granted it was sexy and listening to her had made him unbelievably hot, but still…

Eyes twinkling, she shrugged. "Why not phone sex? It beats checking groceries at the Bag-a-Bargain. It's lucrative, and leaves me time to do the things I enjoy." She gestured around her living room. "Like stained glass, art and gardening." An ironic chuckle bubbled up her throat. "Believe me, I tried other things first. No one wanted to buy my art, and the whole starving-artist gig didn't appeal to me." Her lips curled. "I've grown accustomed to the little things, you know? Food, shelter, electricity." She sighed. "What about you? Aside from tracking down unsuspecting…entrepreneurs, what do you do?"

Will grinned, properly chastised. "I'm a landscape architect," he told her. "Foster's Landscape Design. Almost ten years in business without a single unsatisfied client." Will grimaced as Doris sprang to mind. "At least for the moment, anyway. I'm working with a woman now who might ruin that particular endorsement."

"Oh?"

He rubbed a hand over the back of his neck. "Yeah. Doris Anderson." He gave her the abbreviated version of the past three years, then shared the episode he'd endured this morning. "It's insane. I can't make her happy, can't satisfy her."

Rowan's eyes twinkled with sexy humor. "Sounds like a personal problem to me."

Will blushed, shot her a look from beneath lowered lashes. "That didn't come out precisely right, did it?"

She laughed. "I sincerely hope not." Her gaze drifted slowly over him and she rocked slightly back on the balls of her feet. "*That* would be a tragedy."

Again that little zing of missing excitement buzzed through him and he barely resisted the urge to preen like a puffed-up peacock at the implied compliment. His gaze tangled with hers and he felt a smile flirt with his lips.

"So what are you going to do about her?" Rowan asked, moving the conversation back onto slightly firmer ground.

Will grimaced, passed a hand over his face. "That's the million-dollar question. I honestly don't know." He glanced out her window, then stilled as an inkling of an idea began to emerge. He peered out her window, specifically at the garden framed in the multipaned glass. Another finger of excitement nudged his belly.

What would Doris think of him pulling Rowan in as a consultant? Will wondered hesitantly. For whatever reason, he instinctively knew she'd like Rowan's work. The whimsical layout would undoubtedly appeal to Doris's own fantastical proclivities. In addition, the idea that he'd pulled in another designer to collaborate on the job would appeal to her "special treatment" needs.

Furthermore, he'd gladly forfeit the entire commission to Rowan—who admittedly needed the money more than he did at the moment—simply to make sure that Doris didn't ruin his satisfied customer record.

That he'd be willing to let go with a sizable chunk of change simply to make that woman happy and to keep his flawless record spoke volumes about his control issues, Will knew, but he was powerless to stop it. He'd worked hard for that reputation and the idea that she could ruin it with a few whiny complaints around town—at the country club, specifically—stuck in his craw and absolutely refused to budge.

Not no, but hell, no.

This could work, Will decided, as his idea gained momentum. Doris would get her dream garden, Will would be rid of Doris and Rowan would be able to earn some extra cash doing something she obviously loved instead of keeping up the phone sex gig.

For some unknown reason, the latter perk appealed to him entirely more than it should have, a fact that would need further consideration at a later time.

"Rowan, an idea just occurred to me," Will began, darting her a considering glance, "and I'd like to run it by you."

She nodded. "Er…okay."

Will quickly related his tentative plan, then outlined the offer. "Doris will have to go for it, of course," he qualified. Since she enjoyed being difficult, it would require some fancy footwork on his part, but Will was confident he could bring her around. "At any rate, I honestly think she'll love your work. What do you say? Would you be interested?"

To Will's supreme annoyance a soft chirp sounded from the vicinity of Rowan's waist before she could respond. She tsked under her breath, then tilted a small beeper-sized gadget away from the front pocket of her shorts to better read the display. Her phone, he realized with an unhappy start.

The 1-900-line, specifically.

She winced regretfully, all business once more. "I hate to be rude, but I can't afford to miss this call." She crossed the room, reached out and opened the door for him.

Will swore silently, annoyed at being thwarted this close to what he knew could be victory, and reluctantly made his way onto the front porch. "But, er…what about my offer?"

A mischievous glint lit her gaze and ultimately infected her smile. "You've got my number. Call me."

5

ALEXA PUSHED a hand through her short curly locks and leaned forward expectantly. "Okay, let me get this straight. The kid's uncle tracked you down, showed up at your house today and, after his failed attempt at chewing your ass, he offered you a job?"

Leave it to Alexa to boil her twenty-minute tirade down to a ten-second synopsis, Rowan thought with a droll smile as she dumped a package of peanuts into her Coke. They'd met at Grady's Pool Hall, their usual haunt. The scent of grease and smoke hung in the air, and the continual hum of conversation was broken only by the clack of pool balls. There was nothing chic about the shabby joint, but Grady made the best burgers in town. Contractors, executives, students and locals typically sat elbow to elbow along the battered bar during the day, then the singles crowd inevitably moved in after five. She and Alexa fell among the latter group.

Rowan finally nodded. Her breath left her in a long whoosh. "Yeah, that about sums it up."

Alexa nodded thoughtfully. Her eyes twinkled with do-tell humor and her lips slid into a what-are-you-hiding? grin, a combination Rowan recognized all too well. Their friendship had been forged on the playground to the tune of ring-round-the-rosy, had survived high-school angst and post-graduation blues.

Alexa had nursed Rowan through the broken engagement debacle, and Rowan had returned the gesture following Alexa's nasty divorce. They'd confided every first—first crush, first heartache, first lover—and shared every significant and not-so-significant event in between. They were best buds and, Rowan remembered with a fond smile, they still had the bracelets to prove it.

"That might sum it up—" Alexa leaned back in her seat, pressed her fingers to her forehead and did her psychic-moment impression. Her brow folded in exaggerated concentration. "—but something tells me that you've left a pertinent detail out of your day." She paused. "About this guy, specifically."

Rowan smothered a laugh. Alexa came from a long line of clairvoyants, most recently her mother and grandmother, and despite the fact that the "gift" seemed to have bypassed her completely, Alexa still liked to pretend that she'd been touched as well. Though Rowan suspected that Alexa was secretly relieved that she didn't possess The Sight—often more of a burden than a gift—it had nevertheless been hard for her to come to terms with the fact that she was different from her family.

"Hold on," Alexa said slowly, feigning sudden inspiration. "I'm getting a vision." She nodded, winced, nodded again. "Yes... Yes..." Her eyes suddenly popped open and she grinned. "He's a hottie, isn't he?"

Rowan struggled to maintain a neutral expression, but caved under the unrepentant humor behind Alexa's knowing little stare. Her lips slid into a slow smile and she slumped under the weight of the confession. *"Oh, God, yes."*

Alexa's eyes widened, she whooped with laughter and smacked her hand on the tabletop. "Details," she demanded gleefully. "Now."

Where to start? Rowan wondered as Will's impressive form leaped obligingly to mind. God, she'd never been so affected by a guy. Had never been so instantly—irrevocably—attracted to one. A soft sigh slipped past her lips. "He's tall, tanned, muscled and gorgeous. Tawny hair—lighter on top, darker around the nape." Her gaze turned inward and she propped her chin in her hand. "He's got those heavy-lidded eyes—bedroom eyes—and they're a very light brown, the shade of warm honey," she said, and decided that the description seemed fitting, particularly since she seemed to have gotten *stuck* in that too-sexy gaze.

Alexa arched a brow. "That close, were you?" she teased.

Rowan blushed. "No. Just that…observant," she improvised.

And she'd been observing closely—almost to the point of obsession—though thankfully, he hadn't seemed to notice. She would have gladly continued that covert, narrow scrutiny, too, if it hadn't been for that ill-fated phone call.

Ultimately, she knew the interruption had been for the best. Rowan rarely made snap decisions—she preferred to mull, to ponder, to consider every angle, weigh advantages versus disadvantages and make informed decisions. She wasn't averse to taking risks—calculated ones—when the opportunity arose, but only when she was sure that risk would be worth the reward. Astonishingly, she knew if Roy hadn't called back, she would have readily agreed to Will's offer without the smallest hesitation. Would he be worth the risk? Most definitely. She knew it without a single doubt.

Which just went show how much Will Foster and his sticky-honey gaze had affected her.

Naturally she'd been annoyed that he'd violated

her privacy, that he'd essentially tracked her down with the sole purpose of delivering a load of brimstone with that sexy mouth of his. No doubt he could do it, too, Rowan thought, remembering the grim expression he'd worn when she'd first caught sight of him. After all, she'd noted that intriguing best-friend-or-worst-enemy element of his too-handsome face right from the get-go. Fortunately, she'd had the pleasure of watching that face dawn with the knowledge of his error, then watching that same countenance scramble for, ironically, a face-saver. Her lips twisted with remembered humor.

Listening to the tapes had been just that, she knew. Will hadn't doubted her. He was a smart guy. He'd known that she wouldn't have offered the proof of her statement if she hadn't had the tapes to back it up.

But after all the trouble he'd undoubtedly gone through to run her to ground—honestly, calling a friend in the P.I. business?—he'd had to follow through, or otherwise risk an item men guarded almost as vigilantly as they did their balls—male pride. And women were accused of being stubborn and vain?

Sheesh.

At any rate, Rowan didn't know precisely why she'd been so intrigued by him. Granted, he was gorgeous and, just like any female with working eyesight, the she-woman in her had responded with prompt and primal efficiency when presented with such a fine specimen.

Meaning, she hadn't been remotely inclined to start cleaning his cave…but she certainly wouldn't mind spreading her fur next to his fire.

The idea sent a dart of heat straight to her womb and her toes involuntarily curled in her shoes. A shiver shook her from the inside out, forcing her to exhale a shaky breath.

At twenty-five, Rowan was no stranger to sexual attraction. Promiscuous? No. She'd been very selective with the few lovers she'd had—given the considerable risks that arose when sharing your body it was just plain stupid not to be—but she had enough experience to know that what she'd felt the few minutes she'd spent in Will Foster's company this afternoon was completely out of her sphere of understanding.

The attraction had been more than intense, more than remarkable. It had been fierce and instantaneous—thrilling. She'd *vibrated* with it, felt it echo off her backbone, tingle through her tummy, and most disconcertingly, gently nudge her heart. A heart that had absolutely no business being nudged or prodded or engaged whatsoever. Not after just meeting him. It was crazy. Rowan let go a stuttering breath.

The connection had been curious, to say the least.

She'd been utterly enchanted by him, from his first irate appearance, to that sheepish "I was pissed," confession, then to that ultimate pathetically awkward apology. Clearly he'd been out of his element, but his character had jumped a notch in her estimation with the follow-through. Her lips twisted. Hell, most guys couldn't admit they'd made a mistake, much less apologize for it. That took integrity, a declining quality among today's men, and one she truly admired.

And if those things weren't enough, he was a landscape architect. Her ridiculous heart had actually skipped a beat when he'd confided that little tidbit. A guy who shared the same enthusiasm as she did for the soil, for the science and wonder of gardening? A rare distinction, that. If she'd pulled through a Build-A-Guy drive-through, she couldn't have custom-ordered a better combo. He was smart, funny, into gardening, with Super-Sized sex appeal. A lethal mix to be sure. Quite frankly—probably stupidly—she was fascinated.

"So when do you start?"

Rowan blinked, jolted back into the conversation. "I'm sorry?"

"When do you start?" Alexa repeated. Her eyes twinkled with knowing humor.

Rowan shifted, feigned indifference. "Who said I was going to take the job?"

"Honey," Alexa chuckled with a shake of her head, "*that* was a foregone conclusion."

Rowan tried to muster mild outrage, but quickly felt her expression turn sheepish. She bit her lip, peeked up at her friend from beneath lowered lashes. "That transparent, am I?" She sighed and took a sip of her Coke. Hell, it had been a foregone conclusion. He fascinated her, made her so hot she threatened to burn right out of her skin. Like she could resist that sort of temptation? Like after months of miserable celibacy she would?

Alexa's brow puckered into a thoughtful frown. "Transparent wasn't the word I had in mind—I was thinking more along the lines of *horny.*"

Startled, Rowan almost strangled on a peanut. Her eyes watered as she alternately wheezed, laughed and tried to catch her breath. Geez, nothing like a little truth-therapy from a good friend, Rowan thought, as Alexa silently howled at her expense.

But it would be utterly futile to deny the charge. She was horny. Beyond horny. Succinctly put, something about Will Foster had tripped her trigger. She'd taken one look at him and commenced to simmer. With just a minimal amount of effort on his part, she'd undoubtedly hit a full boil, and just thinking about that kind of singular potential made her loins throb with an achy, hollow sort of heat. Merely imagining that beautiful mouth of his attached to hers, or more importantly, attached to her breast, made her squirm in her seat. Made her fingers itch to slide over that tanned skin, feel those fantastic muscles bunch and flex beneath her hands. He looked fully capable of *satisfying* her, Rowan thought, recalling their previous conversation.

She caught her breath, finally nodded magnanimously. "H-horny works, too," she conceded lightly with a what-the-hell shrug. "What can I say? He's hot…and he makes *me* hot." She grimaced. "That hasn't happened in a while."

Too long to remember, quite frankly. Months. A year, maybe. She'd had a little rebound sex with a former lover after the Mark Mistake, but that had been more about revenge—a stupid reason, but one that had offered a small Band-Aid to her injured pride—and less about her needs. Which was just as well, Rowan remembered now, because she'd had to finish up post-sex while he'd trotted off to the bathroom, completely satisfied. She'd been more miserable *after* the sex than before it.

A shrewd gleam glinted in Alexa's bright blue eyes. "I'm going to make a prediction. I pre—"

Rowan snorted, took another pull from her drink. "Your third eye is blind, remember?"

"I predict," Alexa continued doggedly, "that he'll call you."

Duh, Rowan thought. He'd have to, otherwise he wouldn't know whether or not she planned to come to work for him. "Well, of course he'll call. I didn't give him an answer." She grunted. "If he wants that answer, he'll have to call."

"You're not listening," Alexa chided. "I said, I predict that he'll *call* you," she repeated meaningfully.

They'd established that, Rowan thought, not following. She quirked a brow.

Alexa heaved an impatient breath, leaned forward and lowered her voice. "For phone sex," she hissed, exasperated. She reclined once more, bobbed her head knowingly. "Mark my words. He'll call. He knows what you do, has seen you in action. He's a guy and he'll call. He won't be able to help himself."

Call her for phone sex? Rowan thought faintly. Surely not. For reasons beyond her immediate understanding, the very idea sent a dart of panic directly into her rapidly beating heart. The mere thought of having phone sex with Will Foster made her mouth parch and her pulse race…and not in a good way.

In fact, she felt distinctly ill.

"What?" Alexa asked, seemingly concerned. "What's wrong?"

Though she knew it sounded utterly ridiculous, Rowan blurted out the awful truth. "I can't have phone sex with *him*," she said, her voice equally incredulous and scandalized. "I *know* him."

It was Alexa's turn to wear the uncomprehending look. "So?"

"So, I— I can't do it," Rowan stammered. This was totally bizarre. She hadn't acted like a blushing virgin when she'd been a blushing virgin, and yet...

"Why the hell not?" Alexa scowled, seemingly bewildered. "I thought you just said he was a hottie, that he made you hot. What's the problem?"

"That's the problem," Rowan explained grimly, struggling to find a reasonable voice for her neurosis. "I *know* him," she repeated. "I can't possibly say all those things to him." She affected her phone-sex voice. "*You make me hot. I wanna get naked and touch myself.* Sheesh. Can you imagine, Alexa? I'd be mortified. Don't you see?"

The clank of cutlery hitting the floor sounded to her left. Rowan turned, and from the stunned, gaping looks of the men seated at the next table, they'd obviously overheard her and wrongfully assumed they'd just witnessed kinky lesbian sex talk.

Rowan groaned as humiliation saturated every pore of her face, painting it red. *Embarrassment,* she thought morosely, *my constant companion.*

Alexa smothered a laugh, and massaged her

temples. "Rowan, this doesn't make any sense. You've been pretending for cash with these other yahoos for the past several months, and now you're telling me that you can't do it for real with a guy you're obviously attracted to? Come on," she scoffed.

Rowan winced, conjured a small smile. "Screwed up," she conceded, "but there it is." She paused, vainly searching for the right words to frame her twisted reasoning. "You were right when you'd said I'd been pretending. With other men, it's just a role, Alexa. I can talk some unknown guy through phone sex and not give it a second thought. I'm a catalyst, not a participant. It's not *personal*," she emphasized with a significant look, "if you get my drift."

Alexa's lips rounded in a silent "oh." "You mean you don't actually have—"

"No. No!" she repeated emphatically. She shuddered. "Ick. How could you— I can't believe you thought I—" She shuddered again, stared in horror at her friend. "With strangers? Eeeew!"

"Well, how was I to know?" Alexa defended with an innocent shrug. "I just assumed…"

"Well, you assumed wrong." She exhaled mightily. "Now do you understand?"

"Indeed I do," Alexa replied as a slow smile dawned on her lips. Unrepentant laughter gleamed in her too-perceptive gaze. "The phone sex queen is a phone sex virgin. But I predict a change in status is imminent." She chuckled behind her beer. "This Will Foster is going to pop your phone sex cherry."

Rowan heaved a long-suffering sigh even as a curious thrill followed immediately by a spasm of dread whipped through her. "You and your predictions," she muttered, unable to muster the enthusiasm for a snarky response.

Alexa inclined her head. "I'm right about this one. You'll see. In fact, I would be surprised if you *waited* on *him* to call *you*." She snorted indelicately. "Hell, when have you ever waited for anything you've wanted? Ha! Try *never*." Alexa considered her once more, looked at her until Rowan was hard-pressed not to squirm. "He's really shaken you up, hasn't he? He's knocked you off your game."

Though she knew Alexa was purposely baiting her, Rowan bristled all the same. The mere idea that she was not in control of every aspect of her person, her world and immediate universe annoyed her no end. "I'm *not* off my game." In truth, now that she thought beyond being embarrassed, she could seriously see herself getting into a lusty conversation with Will Foster…and enjoying it immensely.

"Then you're off your rocker. Ordinarily, you wouldn't hesitate, would you?"

"Who said I was hesitating?" Rowan protested. Hell, she wasn't hesitating. She was merely considering. And she was done. If he didn't call her, then fine. She'd call him. Because she *was not* off her game.

WILL DROPPED the phone back into the cradle, exhaled wearily and massaged the bridge of his nose. Well, that had gone much better than he'd anticipated. *That* being, telling Jim about his son's recent moronic detour down the dial-a-date highway.

"You handled that well." His mother appeared from just outside his office door—her favorite eavesdropping post, the eternal infernal snoop, Will thought tiredly—and, with a weary sigh planted herself in one of the chairs flanking Will's desk. "Going to Jim instead of Lori was a wise decision. A boy needs to hear certain things from his father."

Now that was an interesting comment, particularly coming from her, Will thought. Millie had never considered any topic taboo and had never hesitated to share her opinion or advice regardless of the subject. When those ripening teenage hormones had taken hold of him, it had been Millie, not his late father, who'd given him *The Talk*.

That hadn't been all she'd given him either, Will recalled, still somewhat mortified. She'd also given him his first box of condoms along with the sage advice to "bag it before you plant it because a man shouldn't spread his baby gravy over just any biscuit."

His mother, he thought, fondly exasperated…she was one of a kind. The glue that held his tight-knit family together.

"Lying to him wasn't wise," she continued, "but if buying that cock-n-bull story about science lessons gave Jim peace of mind, then so be it, I suppose." She shook her head. "I don't know why people can't face facts but—"

"It wasn't a cock-n-bull story," Will interrupted before she could really get wound up. His mother could spend hours lecturing on the slippery-slope perils of self-delusion. "It was the truth."

Her eyes widened and she blinked. "Says who? Your 1-900-Lover?" she scoffed.

"She'd recorded the conversations. I listened to them." He pulled a negligent shrug, absently drummed a pen against his desk. "No harm, no foul, and she refunded the charges."

His mother hummed under her breath. "Now that's interesting. A *scrupulous* phone sex operator." She smiled, and that shrewd motherly gleam which had unearthed countless secrets flared to life in her gaze. "I'll just bet that threw you for a loop, Mr. Black-and-White."

Will grunted in response to the nickname. His family had called him that for years. As far as Will was concerned, there were no gray areas, period, and people who saw gray simply weren't strong enough in their convictions. He made a decision and he didn't walk the fence.

But had his mother's keen perception once again ferreted out a hidden truth? Will wondered. Had that been why he'd been so fascinated by Rowan? Because he couldn't find a category for her in his black-and-white, right or wrong world? For instance, the idea of phone sex had been singularly unappealing…until he'd met her. Now he couldn't get her voice out of his head, couldn't stop thinking about her saying those erotic little comments to him in that wonderfully sensual voice of hers.

She didn't fit any mold, Will decided. Didn't fit in any of his preformed categories, that was for sure. He'd have to give it further consideration.

But not right now. Not while under his mother's intuitive radar.

He purposely directed the discussion to business, and after the majority of issues were settled, the conversation turned once again to Dreaded Doris.

"What are you going to do about her?" Millie wanted to know. "Honestly, Will. This is ridiculous. You can't call it wasted time because she's always paid you. Still…" She frowned. "Something's gotta give."

Will blew out a breath. "She's connected, Mom. If she's not happy, she's going to howl."

A convenient excuse, one his mother undoubtedly saw through, but he hauled the old line out anyway. She knew how he was. Knew that he couldn't stand the idea of having a single unhappy customer. The idea drove him nuts. Naturally Will knew that it was unreasonable for him to expect to be in any form of public service and never have an unsatisfied customer, but he'd managed to do it for the past ten years—*ten years*—and he simply refused to let Doris Anderson ruin it for him. "I'm working on it," he assured her.

"All right," she sighed, then pushed to her feet. "I'm going to call it a day. Shouldn't you go home and get ready for your date?" she asked innocently.

Will smiled at her tenacity. "I don't have a date."

"Which is precisely my point," she needled with a soft harrumph of displeasure. "Keep it up," she told him as she made her way to the door, "and you're going to end up taking the same dial-a-date detour Scott did."

Will chuckled as he watched her leave, but in truth her parting comment triggered Rowan Crosswhite's last edict, one that had plagued him since leaving her house this morning. It had ricocheted around his brain, pinging him at the most inopportune moments.

You've got my number. Call me.

Will speared his fingers through his hair once more and exhaled a long, pent-up breath.

A simple phrase, a simpler request, and yet he found himself completely stymied, a state that was as annoying as it was unfamiliar. Will prided himself on being a decision maker, on being able to swiftly process data, cull the wheat from the chaff, so to speak, and generally make the right call. This mealy-mouthed do-I-or-don't-I? circle he'd found himself in for the past several hours irritated the hell out of him. It was completely out of character.

But just what the hell had she meant, dammit?

He leaned back in his chair and propped his boots on the edge of his desk. Had she wanted him to call her on her regular line…or had that innocuous little instruction held a double meaning? Had it been a subtle suggestion to dial her 900-line? Or was that merely wishful thinking on his part? Hell, who knew?

Too many questions and not enough answers. A quick glance at his wall clock confirmed that he didn't have much time left either. He didn't know what sort of hours Rowan kept—undoubtedly her phone sex business peaked at night, he thought darkly—but in his opinion anything beyond six implied more pleasure than business.

And, against all reason and better judgment, he wanted both.

The question was; which one did he go after first?

Twenty-four hours ago if anybody had told him that he'd be entertaining the idea of calling a 1-900-number for phone sex, Will would have never believed it. Truthfully, he had trouble believing it now. Hell, he hadn't been a participant in the Five Knuckle Olympics since he'd talked Katie Webber into giving him a hand job in junior high. His lips quirked. After that enlightening experience, self-service had lost its tarnished appeal.

But the mere memory of hearing Rowan's sweet throaty voice made his palms itch and a snaky heat writhe in his loins. Made his imagination run reel-to-reel X-rated material starring her in the lead role, and the idea of listening to her tell him that she was hot made him forget that phone sex surely paled in comparison to the genuine article.

Regardless, he had a feeling Rowan Crosswhite could make a man forget the world was round if she were so inclined.

Though logic and intuition had told him her version of events with Scott had been dead on,

Will didn't doubt for a moment that she could have easily convinced him even without her "proof."

The minute he'd heard her voice the head without the brain had successfully mutinied, and the one responsible for cognitive control had meekly conceded defeat. He'd tracked her down in order to rock her world and, as a result of that infantile arrogance, he'd been the one to walk away shaken and unsure. An unfamiliar condition he'd discovered he didn't care for in the least.

So what to do? Will wondered for the hundredth time. Ultimately, he knew it would be best to err on the side of caution. If she hadn't meant that she wanted him to call on her 900-line, then he'd look like an opportunistic moron, not to mention heartily embarrassed and, though it was vain, he had too much pride to risk the humiliation. In addition, he still needed her help with Doris Dilemma and he didn't want to risk inadvertently pissing her off and nixing that plan.

On the presumption that Rowan would say yes—and he honestly thought that she would—he'd gone ahead and run the idea past Doris this afternoon. Hell, Will thought with a small smile, anyone who thought phone sex was a pragmatic, practical solution to money woes surely wouldn't balk at helping design a garden. Furthermore, he'd seen Rowan's senses go on point, had watched those gorgeous green eyes brighten with excitement when he'd outlined the offer.

Predictably, Doris had balked, but with a little minimal finessing—which almost made him gag—he'd brought her around. The idea of having a special "team manager" had been more than the hard-to-please old biddy could pass up. Now, provided he could bring Rowan on board, everything should be right with his world very shortly. He liked things being right with his world. Anything out of sync—even something as remarkable as this flash-fire attraction for Rowan Crosswhite—messed with his head. Made him antsy. Which meant he needed to grab the bull by the horns, so to speak, and pull himself together.

So, Will decided as he reluctantly sat up, business had to come first…and if he played his cards right, the pleasure would come later.

Luckily, regardless of what line he dialed, he would still get to talk to her, to listen to that sleepy, sultry bedroom voice. The thought had a consoling effect and left him inordinately—ridiculously—pleased.

Which was pathetic and made him wonder just what the hell had been so wrong with his life that a few mere minutes with this woman would make his entire existence seem that much better. Was he that pathetic? Though it galled him to admit it, that lonely? God knew his mother harped on that enough, Will thought, perturbed at the idea. She was constantly going on and on about finding somebody to settle down with. Sharing his life. He chuckled grimly. His mother was convinced that a woman would make him happy, and his sister was equally convinced that having children would humble him.

They acted like he didn't want either, when in truth there was nothing that he wanted more. But he didn't take the decision lightly, and after his last failed attempt at a meaningful relationship, he was a little gun-shy. Deservedly so, if you asked him.

Will cursed under his breath, bullied the thoughts to the back of his mind where he normally kept them. "Idiot," he muttered. "Just call her." He pulled in a bolstering breath and blamed his shaking fingers and quivering gut on low blood sugar as he reached for the phone. He wasn't nervous, dammit. He had friggin' nerves of steel. It was a simple phone call, an offer of employment, one he'd extended countless times.

But for reasons which escaped him, Will instinctively knew he had more riding on this offer than Doris's displeasure, more than a hundred-percent-satisfaction-guaranteed record.

Precisely *what*, escaped him, but the knowledge was there all the same.

He entered her number—for some idiotic reason, he'd memorized it—and waited for her to pick up. After the fourth ring, he knew she wasn't going to answer. On the fifth ring, her machine picked up. Rather than her voice, a Humphrey Bogart soundalike played over the line.

"Of all the answering machines in the world you had to call mine. Maybe the voice messages between two people don't add up to a hill of beans, but if you'll leave me a message, I'll get back to you. Maybe not today, maybe not tomorrow, but someday. Who knows? Maybe this could be the beginning of a beautiful friendship."

Chuckling, Will left his message. Leave it to Rowan not to have a typical greeting on her answering machine, he thought, once again enchanted. Thus far, he hadn't noticed anything *typical* about her. She definitely put the *U* in unique.

Though initially he'd been annoyed—*not* disappointed because that would be just plain sickening—that she hadn't been home, Will decided it was probably to his advantage…because he'd just officially put the ball back into her court. He kicked back in his chair once more, laced his hands behind his head and a slow smile drifted over his lips.

It would be interesting to see what she'd do with it.

6

"SHE SAID CHUNKY MONKEY," Rowan muttered angrily under her breath as she let herself into the house. She slung her purse into the chair by the door, hung her keys on the hook, toed off her shoes, then made her way to the kitchen for a spoon. "I *know* she said Chunky Monkey. The old harpy just wanted my Cherry Garcia."

Note to self, Rowan thought. *The next time I make an ice-cream run, don't make the mistake of showing Ida what I bought for myself.* Better yet, the next time Ida called on her cell phone—man, did she rue the day she'd given *that* number to her landlord, Rowan thought with a grim laugh—she'd simply ignore the call.

She pried the lid off the container, loaded her spoon, then groaned with pleasure as the cool dessert did its magical thing and vastly improved her mood. A Ben & Jerry's antidepressant, she sighed. It did the trick every time.

Honestly, she didn't know why she'd gotten so

irritated. Hell, it was only ice cream. It wasn't like Ida had pulled a playground bully trade, for pity's sake. She still had a dessert, one that she happened to be quite fond of. Good grief. What was wrong with her? If this was the worst thing that happened to her today—Ida stealing her Cherry Garcia—then she was in pretty good shape. Yes, she got sick of running Ida's errands—they were usually mortifying—but it was a relatively easy way to make part of the rent. Sheesh. She had to get a grip.

It was Alexa's fault, Rowan decided as she shoveled another spoonful into her mouth. Her eyes narrowed. Alexa, with her little popping-the-phone-sex-cherry prediction. Rowan knew she hadn't picked out that particular flavor because it was her favorite, or because she liked it above all others—she'd picked out Cherry Garcia because she'd been thinking about Will Foster.

Hadn't *stopped* thinking about Will Foster since he'd left her house this morning.

Would he really call her? she wondered. Her gaze inexplicably slid to her answering machine and a bubble of anticipation fizzed in her belly. Or the better question might be, had he called her? The red light, which signaled a message, blinked furiously, and with a sinking heart, Rowan realized he'd probably already called—and, just her luck, she'd missed it. Damn.

Damn.

Damn.

Damn.

Hauling her dessert along with her, she double-timed it to the living room, sank heavily onto her couch, then pulled the machine into her lap and hit the play button. She winced as her initial fear was confirmed.

"Rowan. Hi, it's Will Foster. I was calling about that proposition I'd run by you this morning. If you're interested, you can give me a call back on my cell or at home." He rattled off the numbers. *"I, uh... I look forward to hearing from you. Thanks. Bye."*

Well, hell, Rowan swore, heartily disappointed. No doubt he'd called while she'd been running Ida's ice-cream errand, she thought uncharitably. In all fairness, he could have called while she'd been at Grady's, but right now laying any and all blame at Ida's hideous feet held considerable catty appeal. Her inner bitch was PMS'ing.

Since he'd taken the first step and contacted her, Rowan didn't see any reason—aside from the herd of butterflies which had taken flight in her belly—why she shouldn't just go ahead and call him. She'd told Alexa she would. Had insisted that she wasn't *off her game.* And she wasn't, dammit.

Furthermore, in an hour or so, her 900-line

would start a perpetual ring, and she wouldn't have time for something as normal as idle chitchat. Even idle chitchat with a guy who made her hormones sing along to the tacky tune of an eighties porn flick. *Chic-a-wow, chic-a-wow-wow,* Rowan thought with a soft chuckle, instantly imagining them in a similar circumstance.

Once again the idea of an intimate conversation with Will Foster took hold. What naughty things would he say to her? Rowan wondered, her belly clenching at the mere thought. Better yet, how long would it take her to make him set himself off? Her breath stuttered out in a quiet hiss and her very bones seemed to liquefy as an image of him doing just that materialized behind her drooping lids. Sweet Jesus. She wanted this guy.

Truly, desperately, with every fiber of her hopelessly horny being.

So she should do it, Rowan decided abruptly, blinking out of her self-induced lust-trance. She should call him. Was going to call him. Right now. He'd offered her a job—admittedly one that she'd love to do, and frankly, she couldn't afford to turn down the money—so there was absolutely no reason to be nervous or nauseous, or be cursed with any shaky affliction. Because that would imply that she wasn't the mistress of her world, wasn't in control and *that* was unacceptable.

Rowan set her ice cream aside, took a deep calming breath, blew it out, then shook the tremors out of her hands. Okay. She was calling. Right now. She picked up the phone and dialed his home number before she could change her mind.

Shit! She'd called him!

"Hello."

Shit! He'd answered! Rowan squeezed her eyes tightly shut. "Er…Will?" Okay, moron, Rowan told herself. Breathe. Hyperventilating over the phone would not help convey the calm, cool, collected chick she longed to portray.

She was *so* not that chick.

"Rowan?"

"Yeah. I was just returning your call." Very good. She didn't stutter, sounded smooth and offhand, as though she weren't pacing the stain off her hardwood floors. She could do this. *Would* do this.

"Right. I, uh— I'd just wondered if you'd thought any more about my offer." He cleared his throat. "If you're interested, I'd like to bring Doris by your place and let her have a look-see."

"Yeah, I'm interested," Rowan replied with a chuckle. "I'm not as sure as you are that she's going to like my garden—my style isn't for everybody— but you're welcome to bring her by whenever. I'm generally home." So she'd see him again. She did a little happy dance around her coffee table.

"Good. I'll give her a call in the morning, and if she's free, we'll probably come by—" he hesitated, evidently trying to figure out his schedule "—er...sometime before noon. I've got my guys started on the tear-out now. She's got friends coming in soon—Peace Corp buddies," he clarified wryly, "and wants to have everything finished, so we're kind of in a time crunch. Is that going to work okay with your schedule?"

Rowan laughed softly. "Hey, I'm basically unemployed, so I'm flexible."

"Good. You're really helping me out of a bind. I'm, uh— I'm at my wit's end with this one."

Rowan didn't get it. If the woman was that damned difficult, why did he keep going back? Why was this satisfaction-guaranteed thing so important to him? Rather than wonder about it, she decided to ask. "Look, it's none of my business, I know, but if she's such a problem why do you keep dealing with her? Why not let it go?" Rowan settled back down on the couch and took up her ice cream once more. She spooned a bite into her mouth.

A rueful laugh sounded in her ear. "I wish that I could, but I... I just can't."

Rowan grinned. Male pride. Was there anything more powerful?

"And, honestly, I can't complain because she's always paid her bill. She's never tried to stick me.

It's just so damned frustrating. She's thrilled, she's ecstatic, she's over the moon—right up until the day we get finished. Then she wants something completely different." He blew out a disgusted breath, punctuating the thought. "You wouldn't believe the work I've put into her damned yard. And all for naught."

Well, that did suck, Rowan thought with a commiserating frown. "So what makes you so sure that she's going to like my garden?" Honestly, if the woman was that hard to please, why *did* he think she'd like her work? she wondered. Why was he so sure?

"Oh, you'll see when you meet her," he readily assured her. "She's a character. Trust me. Your style is right up her alley."

Rowan scowled at the receiver, unable to decide if she should be insulted or flattered. Evidently her lack of response conveyed that message because he quickly moved to fill the yawning silence.

"Damn. That didn't come out precisely right. What I meant is that I think that she'll like your... unconventional approach to landscaping."

Mollified, Rowan felt her lips twitch. "Is that a PC way of telling me that you think my approach to gardening is weird?"

"Nah, not weird." Humor laced his sexy baritone. "Weird has a negative connotation."

Rowan detected the distinct hiss of a bottle being opened, then the muted gulp of a swallow. She found the sound curiously erotic and, to her immeasurable surprise, a flame of heat licked her nipples.

"Unique works," he told her. "Whimsical works better. It's ordered pandemonium, which is completely different to anything I design, by the way, and," he sighed, "is most likely the problem with Doris."

She'd just bet it was different. Though she'd just met him, she could just imagine what he'd design. Lots of symmetrical gardens, regimented lines, plants marching at attention rather than growing at will. Not that there was anything wrong with that, Rowan thought, but it hardly appealed to her.

"Honestly," he continued, "I was impressed. Particularly with your antique roses. Those are a passion of mine as well."

This guy just got better and better, Rowan decided as an unexpected warmth moved through her chest. Well, hell, she thought. He made her warm everywhere else—her chest might as well be infected as well.

She shifted into a more comfortable position and filled her spoon again. "Thanks. I wish that I could take credit for them, but I got them from my mom." She told him about her globe-trotting parents. Rowan chuckled. "She doesn't know it yet, but she's not getting them back."

"Hey, I know what you mean. I've got a Cornelia that I nursed for my grandfather that he's not getting back either."

A Cornelia, Rowan thought, equally awed and impressed. She stilled as something more than sexual attraction, something cerebral went to work on her. So it wasn't just lip service. He really did have a thing for antique roses. Another sparkler of delight ignited in her chest. "I'm envious. I may have to beg a cutting from you."

A deep, sexy chuckle seduced her ear. "Certainly, but only if you're willing to share."

The distinctive ring of her 900-line sounded, interrupting the easy flow of their conversation, and it belatedly occurred to Rowan that she should have turned it off, or at the very least *down,* before she called him. She mentally swore, then smothered a disappointed sigh as a taut silence suddenly hummed between them, a stark contrast to the lively conversation they'd shared just seconds ago.

"Duty calls, eh?" he said. She detected a gratifying hint of disappointment in his voice as well, and something else. Something not easily read. Irritation, maybe?

"You could say that," Rowan replied. The 900-line shrieked again, an insistent reminder that she really needed to let him go. She took a deep breath and strove for a brisk tone. "So I'll see you tomorrow, then?"

"Yeah. Before noon."

"Great. Well…good night."

He barely hesitated, but she felt it all the same. His voice, when he finally spoke, was soft and husky and it made a shiver run through her. "Good night, Rowan."

"YOU WERE RIGHT, Will," Doris told him as she gazed in apparent rapture around Rowan's garden. "*I love it.* I *absolutely* love it. Why, I wouldn't be surprised if a flower fairy suddenly flitted through the air. It's…enchanting," she sighed. "Mystical."

He loved being right, Will thought as he struggled to suppress a smug smile. From the knowing little quirk of Rowan's lips, she'd apparently made that deduction herself. Was he that transparent? he wondered, or did she simply have a keen sense of perception where he was concerned? For reasons he couldn't explain, he got the distinct impression the latter was true. And, astonishingly, he found it singularly…arousing. If she carried that same intuition into the bedroom, he'd be—

"This is definitely what I want," Doris continued, thankfully interrupting him before he could take that thought any further and embarrass himself. "And I'd really love some of those whirly-things, and the stained glass ornaments." She shot Rowan an anxious look. "You can make me some, right?" Doris asked. "They're *fabo. Divine.* I absolutely *must* have some."

"I can," Rowan told her with a quick nod. "Or you're welcome to go through my garage—" She gestured to a building snugged against the back of the property. "—and see if there's anything in there that you like." She chuckled softly. "I've got tons of stuff in there."

Doris's pencil thin brows rose in anticipation. "Oh. Would you mind if I…" She left the rest of the sentence unsaid, but leaned expectantly in the direction of the garage.

Rowan shook her head. "No, not at all. Be my guest. The light's on. I've been out there already this morning."

Will resisted the increasing urge to rock back on his heels. The morning was shaping up quite nicely. Doris liked Rowan's work, which meant a) he'd finally heave that albatross from around his neck, and b) he was guaranteed a minimum of two weeks in relatively close quarters with Rowan. Two weeks to explore this bizarre connection, this phenomenal attraction, to listen to that ultrasexy voice.

Talking on the phone had never been one of Will's favorite pastimes. In fact, he typically hated it. It was a way to expedite information, to increase productivity, to relay pertinent details. Even as a teen, Will hadn't been interested in spending hours on the phone like his other counterparts. Hell, he'd had friends who'd kept the lines tied up for hours at a time simply listening to each other *breathe*. It had baffled him then, and baffled him now.

But a funny thing had happened to him last night—he'd *enjoyed* talking to Rowan. It wasn't just the sound of her voice—though God knows that sweet, sultry nonwhisper did it for him—or the fact that he'd needed to talk to her about Doris—he'd simply *liked* talking to her. It had been easy, effortless, and he thought darkly, he could have undoubtedly continued to talk to her until the wee hours of the morning if it hadn't been for her friggin' 900-line.

It was unreasonable, irrational and all those other adjectives which pertained to his asinine reaction, but Will couldn't seem to help himself. When he'd heard that other line ring, his lips had actually peeled away from his teeth, and every muscle in his body had tensed with equal amounts of irritation and dread.

His response had been swift, irrational and—most disturbingly—telling.

Reason told him that he shouldn't care about what she did, or even who she did it with, for that matter. He barely knew her. Had just met her, dammit. What could it possibly be to him? Logically, he knew that he shouldn't give a damn about what she did on her own time. But there was nothing logical about the way he felt. Nothing logical about the instantaneous attraction he'd felt for her, the keen, almost obsessive fascination.

And curiously, even knowing that she merely talked guys through phone sex—he'd seen her yesterday, and knew beyond a shadow of a doubt that she hadn't gotten one iota of sexual gratification from that conversation with Roy. She'd been *weeding,* of all things. Even knowing that, Will still hated the idea of her talking—*that way*—to another guy. It made his brain cramp. Stupid? Ridiculous? Unreasonable? Definitely. But he couldn't help it.

Thankfully this morning when he and Doris had arrived, he'd noticed, among other things—like the way her shorts hugged her curves, the healthy tan on her slim shoulders, and that ever-present twinkle in those gorgeous green eyes—that the phone and accompanying headset were gone.

Will had breathed a silent sigh of relief and had concluded that, after having a chance to think about his offer and the resulting wage, she'd evidently decided to end her career as a phone sex operator. He couldn't know for sure, of course, but it only stood to reason.

She'd been wearing it yesterday.

She wasn't today.

Ergo, she'd quit.

You could drive a truck through the hole in that shaky self-serving deduction, but until he had proof otherwise, he fully planned to delude himself. It was better for his peace of mind.

And the fact that he had to—or was willing to—resort to such tactics absolutely annoyed the hell out of him. It smacked of jealousy—unwarranted, at that—and he knew from personal experience that that hideous emotion could make a man completely lose control. He swallowed a bitter laugh. His unfaithful ex had been a queen manipulator and the number one tool in her secret bag of tricks had been the green-eyed monster.

To his immeasurable regret, he'd let her drag him around by the short hairs for months. Will was embarrassed to admit how many times she'd made a fool of him, and even more embarrassed to admit how long it had taken him to see her for what she really was—a faithless, self-centered bitch.

Never again, he'd decided.

His gaze slid to Rowan. And yet here he was, infatuated to the point of near obsession. This woman had completely monopolized his thoughts since meeting her yesterday. Yet despite the fact that she was a phone sex operator, of all things, and despite the fact that he barely knew her, somehow Will instinctively knew that she had character.

He saw truth in the determined line of her jaw, sincerity in those frank green eyes and just the smallest hint of vulnerability in her dainty chin. Add hot and sexy, smart and funny to the mix and, well…she became particularly irresistible. He studied the delicate slope of her cheek, the lush curve of her bottom lip and felt a bolt of heat incinerate his groin.

He wanted her.

Another disconcerting realization, but he hadn't *truly* wanted anyone in a long time. Wanted sex? Hell, yeah. He was a man. What man didn't eat, breathe and live for the opportunity of getting laid? Just because he'd bowed out of the dating scene didn't mean that he'd abstained. Getting laid, quite frankly, was easy.

Finding a woman that he really *wanted*, however, was a rarity.

Rowan's gaze swung back to him. Her absolute beauty sucker-punched him once more, and that curious electrical current again raced up his spine.

She smiled and released a small breath. "You're right. She's definitely a character."

"I was relatively certain that she'd like your work," Will replied, swallowing the immediate I-told-you-so that had leaped instantly to his lips.

Perceptive humor lit her gaze. She smiled, crossed her arms over her chest, inadvertently forming an impressive view of her cleavage. "Go ahead and say it," she told him. "I know you want to."

"Want to what?" he asked innocently.

"Say, 'I told you so.'" She laughed. "It's practically eating you up, isn't it?"

"Not eating me up, no," Will qualified. His gaze slid to hers. "However, *I told you* she would like it," he improvised, unable to help himself.

Another sexy chuckle bubbled up her throat. "And you were right. Modesty isn't something that comes easy to you, is it?"

Will laughed. "Not really, no," he admitted with a sheepish grin. "What can I say? I enjoy being right."

"Really," Rowan returned drolly. "I'd barely noticed." She gave him another one of those considering looks, the kind that made him feel like she'd just peeked right into his head. "Why do I get the feeling that being wrong isn't something that happens to you often?"

Will grinned, shoved his hands into his pockets. "Because you're insightful?"

Her delighted laugh made his chest inexplicably swell. "Now that's an interesting compliment," she chuckled.

Will poked his tongue into his cheek. "Thanks. I try."

"I'm sure you do." Her laughter petered out into a soft sigh. "So she likes it. What happens next?"

Ah, the good part, Will thought. "I've got a couple of things that I have to take care of today, but I was hoping that we could use this afternoon to cover some preliminary ground. I thought I could swing by and get you later, then we'd head over to Doris's so that you can get a feel for the size and scope of what you're going to be working on." He covered a nervous sigh with a small cough. "Then, we could either come back here, go to my office…or to my house and get started on the initial layout. We'll need to put in at least a couple of hours, if not more, just so I can go ahead and get a materials list." He blew out a breath. "How does that sound to you?"

"Er… How about I swing by and pick you up," she suggested. "Then we'll check out Doris's, and then we can either go to your house or your office, whichever has the best delivery options." She quirked a brow. "I'm assuming we'll be working through dinner?"

Will laughed. "You're right, we will. Actually, the options are about the same, but we'd probably be more comfortable at my house." Will made a mental note to try and get home early enough to straighten up. She wouldn't be able to find so much as a weed or an uneven blade of grass on his lawn, but unfortunately, he'd never carried that attention to detail into his house. He had a cleaning service come in a couple of times a month, but they weren't due until the end of the week. He inwardly winced. Which meant things were particularly messy.

She nodded. "That sounds fine to me. Just give me a call when you're ready."

Will cast a significant glance at her car parked in the drive and smiled. "Are you going to pick me up in that?"

"No, I thought I'd give you a piggyback ride," she deadpanned, causing a startled chuckle to break up in his throat. She laughed at his frozen expression. "Sorry, I didn't mean to be a smart-ass. Yes, I'm picking you up in that."

Oh, but she did mean to be a smart-ass, Will thought, instantly intrigued as he thoughtfully considered her. For reasons which escaped him, he got the distinct impression that the car was a bone of contention. He didn't know why, but he knew it all the same. "Good," he returned smoothly. "Then I'll look forward to the ride. I bet she's a smooth one." He arched a brow. "It's a '62, right?"

She nodded. "Yep."

"I thought so." He hummed thoughtfully, continued to study the vintage vehicle. Honestly, the car was every man's wet dream and, he thought with a covert look at the woman beside him, *her* behind the wheel made it a double pleasure. "A 327 V-eight?"

"That's right."

"Well, it's gorgeous."

"Thanks."

Will's senses went on heightened alert. Her posture hadn't changed, and she sounded friendly enough, but clearly talking about the car hit some sort of nerve and, though he didn't know where the idea came from, he felt like he'd inadvertently stumbled into some sort of test. What? he wondered. Did she expect him to ask to drive? He suppressed a snort. Like he didn't know better.

That Vette was not the sort of vehicle a person *asked* to drive.

It was disrespectful, not to mention presumptuous, rude and tacky. Had that been why she'd insisted on picking him up? Will wondered now. Or did she merely like to be the one behind the wheel, to literally be in the driver's seat?

He didn't know, but he found himself grimly determined to find out. To solve this little mystery as well. Only one of many concerning Rowan Crosswhite, his principled phone sex operator, he thought with a bemused smile.

His gaze slid to her once more—to her mouth, specifically—and a pulse of heat throbbed in his loins. His mouth parched and his scalp literally prickled with awareness. His palms itched and a sluggish sort of heat wound through his limbs. Need landed another direct hit below his navel and another curious emotion, one not easily read, landed an equally daunting hit in his chest.

Luckily, he could start looking for clues tonight.

7

WILL FOSTER was gorgeous under ordinary circumstances. Will Foster kicked back in her passenger seat—tawny hair blowing in the breeze, slick silver shades over those gorgeous brown eyes, and his long, muscled legs stretched out in front of him—was simply breathtaking.

Since picking him up a little over an hour ago, Rowan had been startlingly aware of him. Every hair on her body had stood on end, a funky quiver had vibrated her belly, and her palms had tingled to the point she'd had to tighten her hands on the wheel to keep from slipping one over his taut thigh.

He hadn't had time to change—in fact, she had the sneaking suspicion that she'd barely beaten him home. She'd caught him shoving an armful of dirty clothes into his kitchen pantry, an act she found stupidly endearing. But he still looked fantastic all the same. Wonderful. Yummy. Delicious.

She'd only been in his house for a moment—the kitchen specifically—but a mere sixty seconds had been enough for her to realize that he didn't concern himself with the finer points of domestication. There were no pictures on the walls, no sentimental bric-a-brac littered about the counter— not so much as a cookie jar—and, horror of horrors, she thought with a small smile, no magnets on his refrigerator.

But despite the glaring lack of decor, the old farmhouse retained a comforting sense of warmth, a cozy ambiance that made her honey-I'm-home fantasy—the one she normally ignored—zoom into Technicolor focus. She could easily see herself in his kitchen, making his house hers and it had absolutely frightened the hell out of her. In a blink of her mind's eye, she'd instantly redecorated the entire room in cobalt blue, pale yellow, red and green. Blue willow and strawberries, toile fabrics and the like. She'd been so caught up in her mental musings that, embarrassingly, it had taken a significant cough from Will to startle her toward the door.

Those melted chocolate eyes of his had danced with a knowing sort of humor, and the corner of his mouth had tucked into a grin that made her alternately want to shrink out of existence and suckle his bottom lip. Her gaze slid to where he sat in the passenger seat.

After spending the past hour in his company,

shrinking out of existence had lost its appeal and the suckling idea had expanded to other areas of his glorious anatomy—the curiously vulnerable patch of bronzed skin behind his ear, for instance. There was something positively adorable—not to mention sexy—about the way his hair curled gently behind his ears.

Yes, to her eternal chagrin and bewilderment, she was looking that closely.

Why? Hell, who knew? Rowan thought, utterly exasperated. But she couldn't seem to help herself. She'd turned into a single throbbing, pulsing nerve of need, and the longer she spent in his company, the more the condition worsened. She wanted him that desperately. More than her next meal. Her next breath.

Even the idea of a virtually unlimited budget and a half acre to landscape in her own unique design hadn't deterred the dogged attraction. If anything, she suspected it had only worsened as a result of it, because now she had more than a serious case of lust going, respect had been thrown into the mix as well.

Landscaping wasn't simply a job to Will Foster, wasn't just a way to earn a living wage—he was truly passionate about it. She'd suspected as much from the beginning, but listening to him talk about sod, fertilizer, trees and flowers while they surveyed Doris's yard had confirmed her earlier opinion. And if that resonating fervor in his voice hadn't clued her in, then one look at his own lawn definitely would have.

Rowan slowed as she neared his house, then guided her car down Will's lengthy gravel drive. The classic two-story house and surrounding property loomed instantly into view, and she found herself just as startled, just as impressed as she had been the first time she'd made this trip.

While he definitely took the minimalist approach to decorating the inside of his house, the outside was another matter altogether. The sloping lawn was graced with mature oak, maple and magnolia trees. Flowering bushes and evergreens hugged the perimeter of the home, and various bedding plants—impatiens, petunias, pinks—lent splashes of contrasting, happy colors to the landscape. Hanging baskets of hot-pink bougainvillea and ivy geraniums lined the porch, and a couple of planters loaded with a variety of flowering plants flanked either side of the front door.

Rowan followed the drive around to the back of the house and found it even more impressive with a second look. A huge antique brick patio butted against the house and surrounded a large kidney-shaped pool with a stacked-stone waterfall. A built-in bar and grill, along with plush patio furniture provided an ample place to simply relax or entertain. Predictably, the entire outdoor room had been accented with lots of greenery and flowers.

In a word, it was gorgeous.

To the left of the pool area, an ivied archway led to a private garden—his antique roses, no doubt—and one she suspected was accessible from the master suite. Though the greenhouse, potting shed and orchard couldn't be seen from the pool area, Rowan had noted them all the same from the road. Every inch of his property had been pruned, clipped, planted and tended with the kind of single-minded tenacity of a passionate perfectionist. She ought to know. It took one to know one, Rowan thought, quelling a grin.

At any rate, recognizing the shared characteristics in him made her chest tingle with a pleased warmth, and her belly clench with another jolt of desire. If he took this kind of care and attention to cultivating a garden, then it simply stood to reason that he'd put that same determined effort into cultivating a lover. The mere idea made her nipples tingle, made her womb quicken. She pulled in a shuddering breath as she shifted the transmission into Park, then let it go with a smile.

"Home, sweet home," Will told her, unwittingly parroting her first thought when she'd walked into his house. "Would you like to have a look around out here before we go inside?"

Most definitely. "Sure, I'd love to."

Time and heat prevented a thorough tour, but her initial impressions were dead-on—he was a perfectionist. She'd also been right about the private garden. His roses were gorgeous, and she made him promise to share several cuttings with her.

Given the perfect state of the yard, Rowan had anticipated a thorough, well-kept greenhouse, but what she hadn't anticipated—an unexpected delight that absolutely thrilled her to her little toes—was his heirloom seed collection. Respect and, curiously, even desire adjusted accordingly.

With the advent of hybrid seeds, many of the open-pollinated varieties were getting harder and harder to find. Hybrids had their advantages, yes. They were disease resistant and consistently produced more uniform fruit and blooms. The trade-off was a lesser scent with the flowers and a muted taste to the fruit, which in Rowan's opinion completely defeated the purpose. Backyard gardeners—like herself, and Will obviously—preferred the nonhybrid varieties. Her gaze slid to Will once more.

Who would have ever thought she'd get this excited over a guy who liked dirt as much as she did? Rowan thought as another flame of warmth tickled her chest and lower extremities.

She fingered a small package of tomato seeds. "Crimson Cushion, Watermelon Beefsteak, Giant Beefsteak and Ponderosa." Impressed, her gaze shot to his. "Wow."

Seemingly uncomfortable, he shoved his hands in his pockets. Soft light filtered through the roof, bathing him in a sepia-looking glow. "It's a hobby of sorts."

It looked like more than a mere hobby to her, Rowan thought, intrigued by his purposely vague description. She picked up a small catalogue. "Some hobby," she said with a small harrumph, for lack of anything better.

Will leaned against a potting table, kicked at a nonexistent rock on the floor. "My father and grand-father were farmers. Farming was too unpredictable for my tastes," he confided with a small smile.

She'd just bet it was, Rowan thought. She'd gleaned enough of his personality to make that deduction in just a few short hours. In fact, Will seemed to enjoy having his way just as much as she enjoyed having hers. The idea that she might have met her match gave her a little thrill, appealed to her more than it should have. "Oh, really?" she asked, tongue in cheek. "I find that hard to believe."

He smiled at her, the grin equally boyish and sexy, endearingly hot. "Yeah, well," he continued. "I still have a healthy respect for it. My grandfather, in particular, was a big proponent of the heirloom varieties." He shrugged lightly, cast a careless glance around the greenhouse. "It's a small way to follow in his footsteps."

Whether it was the offhand way he shared that significant insight—his laudable respect for tradition, or the respect for tradition itself—Rowan didn't know, but her heart inexplicably brightened all the same, and the frightening realization that she could oh-so-easily fall for this guy penetrated her mushy brain and sent a dart of uncomfortable panic right into her overly warm heart.

She'd recognized the Super-Sized attraction. She'd even reluctantly admit to some curiously strong emotions given the short length of time they'd known each other—being with him came easily, made her feel curiously…safe, for a lack of better explanation—but admitting to herself that this could turn into something more than a cavewoman crush was particularly…disturbing.

In fact, though she'd thought she was past the Mark debacle, she suddenly found herself unreasonably spooked.

"Well," Will said, jerking her out of her frown-provoking thoughts. He pushed away from the potting table. "We should probably get started."

"Right," Rowan managed, still unnerved. She pinned what she hoped looked like a natural smile into place and made her way to the door. True to form—getting through a day without embarrassing herself in some way had *never* happened—her sandal caught the lip of the threshold, knocking her off balance and, if it hadn't been for Will's quick reflexes, she would have undoubtedly ended up in a graceless heap face-first, ass-end up on the ground in front of him.

Thankfully, that didn't happen.

Instead, even as her face flamed with a familiar *oh-shit-why-me?* humiliation, another heat spread like a flash-fire over her thighs, up her belly and directly into her breasts. His hands, strong, slightly callused and warm, bracketed her upper arms and her breath left her in a small whoosh as her back came flush up against the hard wall of his muscled chest.

"Whoa," Will chuckled softly into her ear, causing a delicate shiver to dance through her.

Rowan swallowed. Oh, sweet Jesus. His scent, a mesmerizing combination of earth, air and hard work, invaded her nostrils, making her pulse hit an unsteady beat. She made the mistake of shooting an embarrassed glance over her shoulder, and wound up stuck, unable to look away from that warmed honey gaze.

A beat slid into three, and the humor in his eyes swiftly faded, replaced by a heat so intense she barely resisted the urge to melt beneath it.

Every cell in her body sang with joy because she wasn't alone in this unholy attraction—he felt it too. Evidently just as strongly because, thrillingly, a definite bulge nudged the small of her back. His gaze dropped to her lips, an unspoken want she mimicked as well, wordlessly sharing the same desire.

She desperately wanted him to kiss her, could feel that very desire hammering with every beat of her heart, could feel it intensify with every agonizing second that stretched between them.

Then the agony abruptly ended, when he finally swore, then lowered his head and found her mouth with his. There was nothing tentative about the way he took her mouth, nothing hesitant in the way he firmly molded his lips to hers, nothing shy about the bold sweep of his talented tongue into her mouth.

It was hot and delicious, wickedly tantalizing, and the sheer pleasure coaxed an ecstatic whimper from the back of her throat. She turned in his arms, wrapped one hand around his waist, and anchored the other behind his neck, brazenly pressing herself against him. Out of character? Yes, to some degree. But she didn't care because she wanted him and she would do everything in her power to have him. Because it felt right, as natural as breathing. With any other person, she might have hesitated, but not with him. Not with Will. With Will, she could only feel, and the absolute perfection of this moment left no room for modesty, for doubt, for anything but sensation. The burn of desire charred pride and propriety, left nothing but an urgent sense of need.

With a low growl of pleasure, Will sagged against the door frame, pulling her with him. His hot mouth fed at hers even as his hands charted confidently over her back, then settled warmly over her rump. A hot thrill snaked through her at the intimate contact. Her womb clenched with achy need, her nipples pearled beneath the satiny fabric of her bra, and a moist heat coated her feminine folds and swiftly seeped into her panties.

The bulge she'd felt at her back had grown significantly and was now positioned just below her belly button, a pity since she wanted it lodged firmly between her legs. She shamelessly tippytoed, trying desperately to put that part of her that ached the most on a firmer level with that part of him she knew would bring release. Her clit pulsed with an itchy insistent heat, and a tingly warmth concentrated in her nipples as his tongue curled repeatedly around hers. Back and forth, a suckle and a sweep.

God, could he kiss, Rowan thought dimly.

She tangled her fingers into those silky curls at

the nape of his neck, kneaded his scalp and was re-warded with a masculine growl of pleasure. She smiled against his mouth, empowered by the whip of attraction she wielded over him. He tugged her bottom lip into his mouth, and a wave of goose-flesh leap-frogged up her spine, camped in her neck, forcing a preorgasmic shiver.

Will left off her mouth, blazed a trail of kisses down the side of neck. His hands were suddenly everywhere, molding her more tightly to him, reading her body like Braille, drawing sighs and mewls of pleasure from somewhere deep in her throat.

She slid her hands over his chest, felt the mus-cles quiver and jump beneath her palms and, be-fore she thought better of it, had tugged his shirt from the waistband of his pants, then sighed when she finally felt his hot skin against her eager fin-gers. Warm, hot, hard and thrilling…and she wanted more.

Will hummed with pleasure, the sound weaving through her blood, stoking a fever inside her. Not to be outdone, he tugged her shirt down over her shoulder, nipped at her, then tugged it down even more until he bared the top of one breast. He licked a path over the curve of the cup of her bra, then latched his mouth onto her aching peak through the slinky material, unwittingly snatching the breath from her lungs. Rowan arched against him, pushing the needy nipple farther into his hot mouth. Oh, sweet heaven, she thought dimly. She wanted him. Right now.

She *needed*.

With the teeniest bit of effort, she would come right here in broad daylight, fully clothed, in the doorway of his greenhouse.

The idea drew a whimper, another unspoken plea, one that he readily—*thankfully*—interpreted. He shifted, planted his legs farther apart in order to better align their bodies. She literally shook with the anticipation, her insides vibrated with it. She was so very, very close. She tightened her arms around his neck, shifted closer. Closer…

Ahhhh. There.

Oh, God. Please. Almost—

"Will?" a female voice screamed from out of nowhere, practically on top of them from the sound of it, and abruptly cut through the sensual fog surrounding her fuzzy lust-ridden head.

Startled, Rowan squealed and jumped back. Will jumped, too, as though he'd been hit with a cattle prod, then he swore hotly—repeatedly—and squeezed his eyes tightly shut, seemingly trying to summon patience from a hidden source. "Christ," he muttered.

Rowan wiped the back of her hand over her

mouth, darted a guilty look over her shoulder, fully expecting to find the owner of the voice directly behind her. She braced herself for further embarrassment, but curiously, no one was there.

"Will!"

Though she should have been expecting it, Rowan jumped again, squealed. The lips she'd just been kissing tipped into a grin at her reaction. He unclipped his phone—which apparently worked as a two-way radio as well—from his shorts and held it up meaningfully to her. He exhaled a mighty breath. "Yes, Mom?"

Ah. His mother. Rowan bit the inside of her jaw to keep from smiling.

"I tried calling the house, but didn't get you."

His gaze tangled with hers, then he reached out and ran the pad of his thumb over her bottom lip. "That's because I'm not in the house. I'm outside. Was there something in particular you needed?"

"No, nothing particular I guess. I just thought I'd remind you that it's not too late to change your mind about Rebecca Hillendale. I'm sure she'd love to have dinner with you. I could call her back."

Rowan arched a pointed brow and had the pleasure of watching the tips of Will's ears turn red. She kept her expression coolly detached, purposely bored, but inside she writhed with immediate, disproportionate, unfounded jealousy.

She didn't know this Rebecca Hillendale from Adam's house cat, but that didn't keep her from instantly hating the woman, or from forming a less than charitable opinion of her. As far as Rowan was concerned, she was undoubtedly a fat, ugly Class-A bitch and if she knew what was good for her, she'd keep her distance. It was ridiculous. *She* was ridiculous. But she couldn't help herself.

Will massaged the bridge of his nose. "Mom, we've been over this. I'm not having dinner with Rebecca Hillendale. Ever," he added vehemently. "Let it go."

His mother heaved a put-upon sigh. "Oh, all right. But you can't blame me for trying. I don't like the idea of you being lonely."

From the beleaguered look on his handsome face, this wasn't the first time they'd had this conversation. Rowan's intuition went on point. If his mother worried about him being lonely, then that meant he must not date. At least, not regularly. A secret thrill expanded in her chest. But if that was the case, then why? Rowan wondered. Like her, had he been hurt? Or, like so many guys in his generation, was he simply commitment-phobic? Something to ponder later, she decided, filing the information away for future consideration.

"I'm not lonely, Mom," Will insisted. "I'll see you in the morning."

His mother blithely ignored his attempt to end the conversation. "Just because you're not lonely now doesn't mean you won't be in the future—"

Will shot her a long-suffering see-what-I-have-to-deal-with-look and smiled. "I know," he interrupted. "Gotta go, Mom."

"—you know," she continued without the slightest pause. "It's not healthy, a man your age being—"

"Mom."

The pointed edge to his voice finally snagged her attention. "Yes?"

"I'm busy."

Now that was an understatement, Rowan thought with a mental snort, quietly mourning the loss of her almost orgasm.

"Well, you should have just said so," his mother replied primly. "No need to get snippy. I'll see you in the morning."

Will's eyes widened in comical disbelief as she disconnected. "Was I snippy?" he asked. "I don't think I was snippy."

Rowan laughed, shook her head, and crossed her arms over her chest. "Nah, not snippy. Forceful maybe."

Will chuckled darkly. "Trust me. With her, I have to be." A droll smile rolled around his lips. "As you just witnessed, she's not afraid to share her thoughts, opinions or suggestions, particularly when it comes to who I'm dating, or more accurately, *not* dating."

Rowan nodded. "I've got a landlord with the same annoying proclivities. She's convinced I won't be a whole woman until I've changed my last name." She blew out a breath. "It doesn't take long to get old."

He gave her a commiserating nod, then his gaze sharpened. "So you aren't seeing anyone, then?"

Little late to be asking her that, Rowan thought, considering only minutes ago she'd been practically humping him against the door frame—a hot tingle vibrated her belly at the mere thought—but she found herself immensely flattered all the same. She'd detected a hopeful note in his decadent voice, one that made her toes curl in her shoes.

She shook her head and decided a little plain speaking was in order. "No. If I was, I wouldn't have kissed you. What about you?" she asked pointedly, turning the question around on him. "Are you seeing anyone?"

Her bluntness paid off. She watched a glimmer of respect twinkle in those honey eyes, and something else, something just beyond her understanding. His expression wavered between admiration and uncertainty, and a slow smile edged up his lips. "No, I'm not. If I was, *I* wouldn't have kissed *you.*"

She nodded, inordinately pleased, and barely resisted the ballooning urge to bounce on the balls of her feet. For whatever reason, she got the distinct impression that they'd just cleared some sort of imaginary hurdle, stood on the precipice of something new and exciting, slightly terrifying, potentially wonderful.

New romance, she realized with a delighted start. And she hadn't agonized over making the leap.

In fact, she'd done it already—right into his arms.

8

WILL SAT ON his front porch steps and watched Rowan's taillights disappear into the darkness. Sheesh, he thought as he passed a hand wearily over his face.

He was pathetic.

Completely pathetic.

There were a half-dozen things that required his immediate attention, and rather than briskly tending to them as he normally would, he'd parked himself on the porch—in the dark, no less—to mope over Rowan's premature departure.

In truth, there was nothing premature about it— they'd been working for hours. It was late. She'd needed to go home. Were he capable of being logical, he'd understand that. Regrettably, the logical part of his brain—the part that ordinarily maintained control—had been short-circuited by single-minded selfishness and a virulent, almost debilitating case of lust.

In fact, Will thought, still unreasonably annoyed, if it had been up to him she wouldn't have left at all. She'd still be seated at his dining room table, poring over designs and catalogues, enthusiastically talking about her plan for Doris's yard in that erotic almost-whisper of hers that made his scalp prickle and his dick strain against his zipper.

She'd be laughing with him, sharing anecdotes and gardening tips. She'd be keeping him company, making this big old house feel a little smaller, a little warmer simply because she was in it. And though he knew it was the most ridiculous thing in the world and it galled him no end because it demonstrated a lamentable lack of control, he found himself curiously reluctant to go back inside, into his own damned house. Why? Because she wasn't there, and he instinctively knew he'd feel the absence more keenly.

How screwed up was that?

Hell, he'd dated. He'd even had the occasional overnight lover, though quite honestly he'd never been completely comfortable sharing his bed *after* sex. Ironically, it felt too intimate, too personal. There was a vulnerability in sleep that required a certain level of trust.

He'd made the mistake of trusting someone once and the outcome had been ruinous.

Naturally, Will knew that it was unfair to paint

every woman with the same rotten brush, but his confidence had been badly shaken. He grimaced. Not being able to trust a significant other was disturbing, but not being able to trust your own judgment was considerably worse. He watched a moth flutter around his porch light and absorbed the truth of that statement.

But despite his hang-ups and reservations, Will instinctively knew that he could trust Rowan. He didn't know where the knowledge came from—call it intuition, ESP, whatever—but after less than twenty-four hours in her company, he knew it with a certainty that defied reason and trumped doubt.

From the moment he'd heard her voice—*just her damned voice*—he'd been instantly enchanted. He'd been drawn to her in a way that defied explanation, and every second up until this very minute had reinforced that initial reaction.

Then he'd kissed her and, for all intents and purposes, his world had tilted on its axis, the sky had fallen and time had stood still.

A residual quake shimmied through him at the mere memory, forcing him to expel a shaky breath. Heat stirred in his loins and his fingers involuntarily flexed against his palms.

To be honest, Will had been secretly delighted when she'd tripped—it had given him a reason to touch her—and, though he'd fully intended to kiss her tonight, he hadn't planned on making his move until after their initial work on Doris's design had been finished. Though she had to know that he was attracted to her—she was damned perceptive, after all—he hadn't wanted to seem too transparent, too eager or, God forbid, too needy.

But the moment he'd touched her any preconceived notions of propriety or neediness had fled instantly from his head, burned away by a shock of heat so intense he'd almost staggered from the voltage. The feel of her body pressed against his had been painfully sweet, sinfully erotic…inexplicably *right*. He'd gone from semiaroused to rock-hard in a nanosecond, then she'd turned her head and… Will expelled a long breath.

And he'd been lost.

One look into those gorgeous green eyes—honestly, he'd never seen a shade as compelling as hers—and he'd lost the battle. They were true green, the bright, hopeful color of a new leaf, and that hue coupled with that rueful embarrassment and her wobbly smile had positively sent him over the edge. He'd watched heat chase away her humiliation, then her gaze had dropped to his lips and, lowering his head—finding her mouth—at that moment had seemed as necessary as breathing.

Now, perversely, he felt like he'd suffocate if he couldn't do it again.

Kissing her had been the closest thing to a spiritual experience Will had ever had. Every hair on his body had stood on end, his pulse had tripped, his breathing had gone shallow, and a curious roaring had commenced in his head. She'd tasted like peppermint and fresh peaches, like a sweet rain after a long drought. He swallowed. Like hope, a kept promise, an unexpected gift.

Her lush frame had molded to his effortlessly, as though her body had been specifically tailored and designed to fit his. Will had never believed in "perfect." Like love, it was a word that had been thrown about and overused until the meaning had been diluted, bastardized. Until today, he'd never experienced anything even remotely close to what the true meaning of the word implied...but there was simply no other way to describe the way she'd felt in his arms, the way she'd tasted against his tongue.

That had been flawless.

He wanted her with an intensity that was frightening. Missed her, dammit, of all things, and she'd barely been gone twenty minutes. If he felt this strongly now, just what the hell would happen to him *after* he took her to bed? It was too disturbing to think about, so he firmly closed the door on that line of thinking—as a guy, he was wholeheartedly opposed to thinking/talking about feelings—and instead concentrated on a much more pleasant notion—planting himself between her thighs. Will grinned.

If kissing her turned him inside out, then plunging into her tight, wet heat would undoubtedly rock his world, and God, how he looked forward to the quake.

Tasting her mouth had only been an appetizer, a prelude to the grand event. He couldn't wait to sample her breasts, to feel those tight buds which had raked across his chest this afternoon pebbled against his tongue, flattened against the roof of his mouth. Couldn't wait to slip his fingers between her thighs, then his tongue, and sample the sweet nectar hidden in that secret valley.

A painful ache built in his loins and his breath hissed out between his clenched teeth.

God, he wanted her.

Right now.

Will didn't know where the idea came from, what maggot had taken hold of his brain, but before he could question what he was doing, he strode into the house and dialed her number. Since he'd acted without thinking, he was at a complete loss when she answered the phone.

He squeezed his eyes tightly shut and swore under his breath. "Er…Rowan." Brilliant. Just freakin' brilliant. He sounded like a complete moron. What in God's name had possessed him to call her?

"Will?" she asked uncertainly.

He plopped into his recliner and racked his brain for any plausible reason as to why he'd be calling her when she'd just left his house a few minutes ago. What the hell could be so important that it couldn't wait until tomorrow morning, when he'd see her again?

They had to meet with Doris for design approval—and this time he planned to get something in writing so that she couldn't change her mind again—then, once she signed off, they planned to mock the hardscape into scale so that the next phase could begin.

"I, uh…" *I'm so friggin' pathetic that I just wanted to hear the sound of your voice.* "I forgot to ask," he said, conjuring a brittle laugh. "Who's picking who up in the morning?"

She hesitated, clearly baffled because they'd gone over that right before she'd left. "Er…you're picking me up."

He rested his elbows on his knees, rubbed the bridge of his nose. "Right. That's what I thought."

This was ignorant. He needed to just lay it all on the line.

Will slouched back into his chair, blew out an exasperated breath. "Look, I knew that. That's not the reason I called. To be honest, I have no idea why I called. I just—" He paused, searching the quagmire of his brain for the right words. "I just really enjoyed tonight, more than I've enjoyed any-thing in a long time, and I— I wasn't ready for it to be over. Can you talk for a while? Do you *want* to talk for a while?" Christ, did he really have to sound so damned desperate?

Several nerve-racking seconds ticked by before she responded, and when she did, her voice held a warm but strangled quality. "Sure, I'd love to. But would you mind if I called you back in a few min-utes? I've got a couple of things I need to take care of first."

Will breathed a small sigh of relief. "Sure. Just give me a call back when you're ready. I'll, uh…" He cleared his throat. "I'll be waiting."

ROWAN DISCONNECTED. A slow smile rolled around her lips and the tingly feeling of joy she'd carried home with her tonight multiplied until a giddy burst of laughter bubbled up her throat and she did a little happy *Lord of the Dance* jig around her liv-ing room.

Okay, okay, okay. She stopped, pulled in a deep calming breath and tried to act like a rational adult.

The problem was she didn't *feel* like a rational adult. Rational adults didn't skip around their living room simply because a guy had called and said he'd had a good time with her. Rational adults didn't smile like a donkey with a mouthful of briers for no particular reason, and rational adults didn't absently chew on the phone antenna to keep from squealing with delight.

Rowan knew to an uninformed bystander, she'd look like a schizophrenic who'd just gone off her meds, but there was one person who would understand how she felt right now and that person had left a message on her machine, and was the sole reason why she'd insisted on calling Will back instead of continuing to talk to him—Alexa.

She toed her shoes off, hit speed dial and, while she waited for Alexa to pick up, she made her way to the back of the house to change clothes.

"Well?" Alexa demanded when she answered. "How did it go?"

Rowan shimmied out of her shorts. *"It was fantastic,"* she said, drawing each word out for maximum impact.

Alexa squealed. "I knew it, I knew it. I had a feeling about this guy. Tell me everything. Start at the beginning and don't leave anything out."

Rowan kicked her shorts aside, then rummaged through a drawer until she found a nightgown. "Hold on a minute." She tossed the phone onto the bed, shed her shirt and bra, then quickly tugged the nightie over her head. It settled coolly over her skin.

Ah. Much better.

She didn't know what sadistic mind had invented the bra, but she'd be willing to bet the damned torture device had been a man's idea.

Rowan snagged the phone once more. "Okay. I'm back."

"What the hell were you doing?"

"Changing clothes."

"So?" she asked meaningfully. "What happened?"

"I've only got a minute—he's called and I've got to call him back—so I'll have to give you the abbreviated version."

An exasperated huff sounded in her ear. "Fine. I'll just ask a couple of questions, then. One…did he kiss you?"

Rowan melted onto the side of her bed. Oh, God had he ever. "Yes, he did."

Alexa whooped into her ear. "Okay," she said with a delighted laugh, "the sound of your voice answered question number two, so I get another one. Did he at any time ask or imply that he'd like to drive the car?"

A flutter of warmth tingled beneath her breast. "No, he did not." He'd complimented the car, her handling of it, specifically, then he'd stretched those gorgeous legs out in front of him, simply sat back and enjoyed the ride.

"Well, there you go," Alexa said matter-of-factly. "We've got a winner."

Rowan silently agreed. Especially if tonight were to be any sort of indicator. Everything about this evening had been absolutely wonderful. From the moment she'd picked him up, to that scorching, belly-clenching good-night kiss, and every second in between, the entire night had been beyond fantastic.

Finding the strength to get into her car, when she knew that he'd wanted her to stay—and more importantly that *she'd* wanted to stay—had been one of the most difficult things Rowan had ever done. Even now, she couldn't say precisely why she knew it would be best to leave, but she'd known it all the same, and since her disastrous engagement, she'd never been one to ignore her instincts.

Physically, she was ready. She barely suppressed a snort. Couldn't be any more ready. Was beyond ready. Mentally, though, for whatever reason, she simply hadn't arrived. But it was only a matter of time, and a short one at that. She knew it, could feel it.

I'll be waiting.

A shiver went through her, remembering the heat in that curiously vulnerable, sweetly poignant murmur. Three little words, and yet more meaning and promise lurked in that simple succinct phrase than she could have imagined.

Shit, she thought with a mental duh. *He was waiting.*

She scrambled from the bed, quickly related this to Alexa, and promised to call her tomorrow with more details.

"Wait! Wait!" Alexa shrieked before Rowan could hang up."

She hesitated, slightly perturbed. "What?"

"Don't forget to turn off your 1-900-line," she advised sagely.

Oh, hell, Rowan thought. That could have been a disaster. "Right, thanks."

"I mean, you'd hate to have your phone sex line ring and interrupt your ph-phone sex." Alexa giggled maddeningly. "That would be tragically ironic, wouldn't it?"

"You're twisted," Rowan scoffed, even as a wriggle of something slightly wicked tripped up her spine. Her belly trembled, but not with fear. With anticipation. "Who said anything about having phone sex?"

"Nobody has to…but you can kiss your cherry goodbye, Virgin-Girl, and my money's on tonight."

"We're just going to talk." A token protest, she knew, but one she felt compelled to make anyway. Quite frankly, after that wonderful kiss, almost orgasm, then fantastic dinner where, despite the fact that they'd gotten their work done, every word had resonated with sexual innuendo, Rowan was ready for a little sexy wordplay. To hell with being embarrassed. She was too damned hot.

"Yeah, right. About having sex—"

Rowan rolled her eyes. "Shut up."

"—with each other."

Rowan grinned. Alexa was incorrigible. "I'll call you tomorrow."

As Alexa had so fortuitously pointed out, Rowan booted it to the living room and turned off the ringer on her 1-900-line. She normally tried to keep the same hours—the majority of her clientele were repeat callers—but tonight they'd simply have to do without her. She'd take a B-12 vitamin, and make up the time once she and Will were finished with their…conversation.

Quite honestly, in light of what she'd make from the landscaping job, Rowan had been seriously tempted to disconnect her 900-line—that job alone would float her through until her teaching contract was renewed—but then she'd imagined the big goose egg in her savings account and the balance on her student loan debt, and practicality had won out. She made a moue of disappointment. Given her recent financial straits, she couldn't justify cutting off *any* income. It simply wasn't prudent.

So, while she had the opportunity, she'd decided that she'd be better off to net as much money as she possibly could so that if, God forbid, she ever found herself unemployed again, she wouldn't end up in the lamentable shape she'd been in this time. She'd narrowly missed having to ask her parents for help, and quite honestly, she'd rather be eviscerated with a rusty blade.

Unlike her brother, *she* would not be a source of disappointment.

She would take care of herself.

And if phone sex was what it took, then so be it.

And speaking of phone sex…she needed to call Will back. As for whether or not Alexa's prediction would come true, Rowan couldn't say. Her belly vibrated with anticipation at the mere thought and her feminine muscles clenched, forcing her breath through her lips in a shaky, nervous hiss.

But curiously, what had literally scared the bejesus out of her yesterday didn't seem frightening now and she suspected the antidote had been administered during that inferno kiss this afternoon. *Mama mia,* Rowan thought as remembered heat licked her nipples. Hell, who had time to be nervous? She was too damned horny.

Pop her phone sex cherry, indeed, Rowan

thought as she punched in Will's number. Her lips slid into a slow grin.

One could hope.

9

WILL BLEW OUT an impatient breath and quietly watched another minute blink past on his VCR display. A screw of unease tightened in his chest. She'd asked for a few minutes. As far as Will was concerned, *a few* implied three to four—five at max.

He'd been waiting for six and every second that had passed in between had felt like a damned eternity, providing him with ample time to second-guess the merits of placing that last call.

Had she changed her mind? he wondered now. Had he frightened her off? I mean, honestly, Will thought, silently cursing himself. She'd just left—had just gotten home—and rather than playing his cards close to his vest, or trying to maintain even the slightest semblance of control—or pride for that matter—he'd pounced on her the second she'd walked through her damned door.

Will's eyes widened. Oh, *hell.* He'd screwed up. A grim chuckle burst from his throat, and a hot poker of stupidity prodded him in the ass, forcing him to leap to his feet. He paced the area in front of his favorite chair, speared his fingers through his hair.

Shit, shit, shit.

He'd screwed up. He shouldn't have called her, he thought faintly. What in God's name had he been thinking? Hell, he hadn't been thinking, Will thought with a miserable groan of disbelief. Hadn't been able to use anything which remotely resembled his so-called gray matter since he'd heard her *voice* yesterday. *I had a good time, and I wasn't ready for it to be over?* Mortification scalded his cheeks, burned the lobes of his ears.

It was the attraction, Will decided with a fatalistic grunt. It had obviously flambéed his brain. There could simply be no other explanation for his over-the-top senseless, moronic, out-of-character behavior.

Clearly, he'd lost his mind.

Lay it all out on the line, indeed, Will thought now, feeling beyond ridiculous.

He'd laid something on the line, all right—his ass. The ass he wished he could kick himself. He swore again and expelled an exasperated breath. Good grief, would he ever learn? Would he ever—

The ring of the phone cut through his self-recriminations. He stopped midstride, and his gaze swung to the phone. Every ounce of worry evaporated as a profound relief saturated every cell in his body. His shoulders slumped and he passed a hand wearily over his face.

Okay. So maybe he hadn't screwed up.

He quickly crossed the room and snagged the phone. "Hello."

"Hey, sorry I took so long," Rowan told him. "I had to return a call—my friend Alexa had left a message—and I wanted to change clothes." She sighed into his ear. "You know, get comfortable."

In other words, she'd shed her bra. His mouth parched at the very idea, making his voice slightly rusty when he spoke. He sank into his recliner. "Yeah, I know what you mean."

She laughed. "So you got comfortable, too?"

Will smiled, glanced at his discarded clothes piled in a messy heap next to his coffee table. Hell, it was too damn hot to stay fully clothed. "I guess you could say that."

"Let me guess," she told him, humor lacing that erotic voice. "Your shirt, shoes and socks are sitting in a pile on your living room floor."

Will didn't know whether to be alarmed or impressed, so instead he chuckled. "How'd you know?"

"Because you haven't had time to take them to your pantry yet."

A startled chuckle burst from his throat. Oh, wow, he thought. Busted. "You saw that, did you?"

Will asked, somewhat embarrassed. He picked at a loose thread on his shorts.

"I did," she laughed. "Sorry. I shouldn't have said anything."

"Nah," he told her. "Don't worry about it. Hey, what can I say? Keeping up the house isn't one of my strong suits. I'd rather be outside."

Her laughter tittered out into a soft sigh. "I know what you mean. Your place is gorgeous, your rose garden in particular. I'm truly envious."

"Thanks. A lot of work goes into it, but it's worth it. And yours is nothing to sneeze at," he told her. "You've done an amazing job." Particularly considering she'd had no formal training. Honestly, he'd love to add her to his team permanently. It was something to think about, at any rate.

Her voice grew warm. "I do love it. There's something so therapeutic about gardening. I love planning and planting, watching my babies grow and bloom."

"And don't forget weeding," Will reminded her magnanimously. "You're a—" He laughed, he couldn't help himself. "You're a champion w-weeder." Will didn't have to see her to know that her face had undoubtedly turned bright pink.

Several beats passed, then, "I'm never going to live that down, am I?"

Still smiling, he sighed and absently scratched

his chest. "Probably not. I know I'll certainly never forget it." And he wouldn't. Listening to that sweet throaty voice rise and fall, pant, sigh and moan in orgasmic simulation was indelibly imprinted on his brain, on his eardrums. He'd mentally edited the scenario, had replaced Roy's name with his own, and played it back in his head whenever the urge struck. Which was frequently.

"Well, I wish you would," Rowan said, slightly exasperated. "It wasn't one of my finer moments," she said drolly.

Will quirked a brow. "Really? I was impressed."

She harrumphed. "Well, I can do better."

Will stilled as her unspoken oh-shit hummed between them. He instinctively knew that she'd blurted that out without thinking, and a nice guy— a less horny guy—would undoubtedly let it slide without comment. Unfortunately, the idea that she could do better than what he'd heard yesterday had taken root between his legs and, rather than letting her off the hook, he wanted to make her wriggle for a little while first.

He cleared his throat, lowered his voice. "Do better, huh?"

An audible swallow sounded in his ear, making his smile a smidge wider. "Well…yes, actually."

Too much pride to back down. When push came to shove, this was a chick who'd put her money where her mouth was. An admirable quality, that, Will thought, unreasonably impressed. Besides, he liked the direction this conversation was taking. He reached down and adjusted himself. It lessened the room in his shorts.

"I'd like to hear that," Will told her. "Care to give me a little demonstration?" he asked lightly.

She chuckled, the sound at once sexy and sweet. "Sounds like you're asking for a freebie."

"No, of course not," Will readily replied. He laughed. "That would be tacky. You're the one that said you could do better. I'm merely curious is all."

"Oh, well," she said, humor tingeing that sultry nonwhisper. "If that's the case, then that's different."

"I thought so."

"So, what do you want?" she asked. "Just a straight orgasm, or would you like the works? The whole, I-want-to-get-naked-and-touch-myself-because-you-have-the-biggest-rod-I've-ever-seen-and-only-you-can-make-me-sing-the-Hallelujah-chorus spiel?"

Will blinked drunkenly. Just like that, he lost the upper hand. His smile slowly faded and every ounce of blood raced from his extremities and pooled into his loins. His tongue felt huge. "Wha— Whatever you think is best."

"You fed me this evening," she said, an implied shrug in her voice. "I guess I could give you the whole spiel, but it's going to require a little effort on your part." He got the distinct impression that she was laughing at him, that he'd somehow prodded her into this course of action. "Are you up for it?"

He cleared his throat again, considered just how friggin' *up* he was and barely swallowed an ironic grunt. "Sure. Yes. Of course."

"Good. Then let's pretend that you've called me, okay? We're going to take it from the top. Are you ready?"

This time he did laugh. "Oh, yeah."

"Good… *Hello.*"

The difference in the tone of her voice was staggering. Low. Husky. Rife with the promise of a wet dream, and he felt it eddy through him. She was *on,* Will realized. She was ready to play her part.

But he didn't want her just to play her damned part—he wanted her to participate.

If he'd learned one thing this afternoon, he'd learned that she wanted him every bit as much as he'd wanted her. She hadn't merely kissed him— she'd devoured him, had practically tried to crawl up under his skin. She'd been a slave to the attraction just as much as he had.

So why the ruse? Will wondered. What was she afraid of?

He didn't know, but it damn sure wasn't going

to be him, and he wasn't going to allow her to turn him into another Roy. His lips tightened.

Not no, but hell, no.

In fact, though now was not the time to ask her, he sincerely hoped there were no more "Roys."

Two could play at this game, Will decided, and while she had the benefit of experience, he had a hard-on that could up-end a Mack truck. In addition to that, he knew her, and he fully intended to press that advantage. He'd noted what had turned her on this afternoon, had committed each and every sibilant sigh and hiss to its coordinating erogenous zone.

So bring it on, Will thought. He was ready to rumble.

ALEXA HAD BEEN RIGHT—she was about to lose her phone sex cherry.

Rowan's heart raced, her mouth parched and a tingly heat concentrated at the apex of her thighs. She didn't know what had possessed her to tell him that she could do better—vanity perhaps, because she knew that she could. She'd been in a hurry that day. But regardless of why she'd said it, the boastful retort had had the desired effect because she and Will Foster were about to scorch the phone lines. She could feel the heat already. Looked forward to the burn.

His voice, when it finally came, was every bit as low and seductive as hers had been. "Hi."

Rowan sank her teeth into her bottom lip. *Oh, yeah,* she thought. *Here we go.*

She made a valiant effort to catch the thread of the conversation. "I'm glad you called," she murmured. "I've been lonely." A standard response, but this time the line rang with a hint of truth that made her swallow.

His soft chuckle seduced her ear. "Lonely, eh? That's a pity. I'll try to do something about that. I haven't caught you at a bad time, have I?"

Rowan shifted against her sheets. "No, I'm just lying here all alone in my big old bed." She purposely lowered her voice, injected that sultry quality that never failed to elicit a response. "What about you? What are you doing?"

"I've been thinking about a girl I met yesterday. Thinking about her a lot, actually."

Her heart rate shifted into overdrive, threatened to beat right up out of her throat. Oh, no. He wasn't following the script. "You have?" Did that thready voice belong to her?

"Yeah, she's pretty damned hot, and she's got this voice that makes me swell out of the top of my shorts. It's soft and husky, sleepy almost. One of those bedroom voices, you know? I've never been so attracted to another person. *Ever.*"

A bud of pleasure bloomed in her chest and, impossibly, another dart of warmth penetrated her womb. "We've got something in common then, because I've found myself in a similar situation recently. I met a guy yesterday and…*my God.*" She slumped against the back of her bed. "He's gorgeous. He's got the most amazing mouth. It's a little full for a guy, but so damned sexy it makes me…wet. Makes me fantasize about kissing him…and having him kiss me…in lots of different places."

She paused, imagined him kissing her right then. Could practically feel his lips melded to hers, the evocative thrust of his tongue into her mouth. Her breath left her in a stuttering whoosh. "In fact, he kissed me today and I came within a gnat's ass of one hell of an orgasm." She winced. "Unfortunately we were interrupted." Rowan felt her lips tip into a grin. "His mother called."

His voice had developed a rasp. "That was unfortunate."

"I'll say," Rowan readily concurred. "We'd been standing against the door frame of his greenhouse—he's a dirt freak like myself, which makes him all the more attractive, I might add—and," she sighed, "if it hadn't been for that fateful call, I'm certain we would have done it right then. I wouldn't have been able to say no, that's for sure. I wanted him. Desperately."

A stuttered breath hissed across the line. "I know what you mean. I want this girl pretty damned badly, too. She's…amazing. I kissed her today, and…*mercy.* Every thought drifted right out of my head and I literally tingled. My palms itched so much that I couldn't keep my hands off of her. I slid them over her ass—did I mention that she's got one helluvan ass?—and… *Wow.* I narrowly avoided embarrassing myself, that's for sure. But I just can't help it. I *want* her and I haven't wanted anyone in a long time." He sighed. "Too damned long."

Rowan absorbed the compliment, smiled as lust and delight commingled in her belly. "So, do you think you and her will get together?"

"Most definitely. It's inevitable." She heard the smile in his voice and just enough confidence to be arousing. "I'm just waiting for the right moment to make my move."

A steady throb built between her legs and her nipples pearled against her nightgown. If she'd ever been more turned on in her life, she couldn't recall it. Need was a living breathing thing inside her, consumed her to the point of complete distraction. "If you—" She moistened her lips. "If you could have her right now, what would you do to her?"

His laugh was rife with anticipation. "First, I'd draw her hair away from her neck—she's got long, gorgeous hair. Very sexy. Makes Lady Godiva look like a troll—then I'd kiss that tender part of her throat where her neck meets her shoulder. I touched her there today, and she melted against me, so I know she'd like it."

Rowan hummed. She knew precisely where he was talking about and the fact that he'd noticed how much she enjoyed it was singularly arousing. Made her wonder what else he'd noticed about what pleased her. Her lids drooped. "Go on."

"I'd like to say that I'd take my time making love to her. That I'd take things slow and easy, savor every second." He sighed softly and she felt that whispery sound simmer in her blood. "But I want her too badly, and the first time, I know I simply wouldn't be able to hold back. I'd devour her. I'd get her naked as swiftly as possible, then I'd lick, suck, kiss and nuzzle every inch of her in short order."

His voice was smooth, yet lightly rough. Like the slide of denim over silk.

"Her breasts are full and ripe, and I felt her nipples against my chest this afternoon." He hissed. "It nearly killed me. I wanted to feel them in my mouth, wanted to taste them so desperately. I'd have to linger around them for a few moments. Flick them against my tongue. Back and forth, then latch on again. Do you think she'd like that?"

Oh, God, would she ever. What he'd described

was right in keeping with her own thoughts. She wanted him to devour her. Wanted him to lick, suck, kiss and nuzzle her. Wanted his hot mouth anchored at her aching, pouty breasts right now. Like he'd done this afternoon through her bra.

Rowan couldn't help herself, needed some small amount of relief. She let her hand drift over one breast, over one distended nipple, winced, then relieved the other one as well. Her blood sizzled. "She'd...like it," Rowan managed to croak brokenly.

"Good." His voice had developed a rasp. "I'd— I'd thought so."

"What would you do next?" When had she become such a glutton for punishment?

A sexy laugh resonated into her ear. "Oh, I'm glad you asked. Next, I'd kiss my way down her belly, then I'd hook her legs over my shoulders and feed at her—fast, remember, because I'm not strong enough to wait—until I made her come and had sipped up every last ounce of her release."

The vision materialized so swiftly behind her lids that she gasped and slid her hand down over her muddled belly. She edged her gown up, dallied beneath her drenched panties. Her back arched away from the bed as pleasure bolted through her.

"Then, once she'd melted for me once, I'd slide right into her wet, tight heat, and pump in and out of her until she did it again." His breathing grew ragged and he seemed to snap under the strain of their sexy wordplay. "Can you feel me there, Rowan?" he whispered. "Tell me you feel me."

"Oh, God yes," she gasped, working her tender flesh beneath her frantic fingers. "Can you feel *me?*" she asked. "I'm clenching around you because every time you retreat, I want to draw you back in. I'm on fire and I— " She gasped as the sharp tug of beginning climax ripened in her sex.

She heard a muttered curse, then a hiss of relief which told her he'd taken himself in hand. The erotic image burned into her brain, made a broken laugh of relief shimmy up her throat.

"Oh, God," she panted. She rolled her head from side to side, barely had the strength to hang on to the phone. Though she knew it was impossible, she could feel him there between her legs, had *felt* every sensual treat he'd described. His hot mouth suckling her breast, that blond head licking a path down her belly, then greedily feasting between her thighs. Then the long hard length of him filling her up, satisfying that itchy, achy heat centered deep into her womb. "I need— I want—"

"Tell me what you want, baby, and I'll give it to you," Will told her.

"Harder," Rowan gasped. "Faster." She upped the tempo, imagined him plunging in and out, in and out, until finally—blessedly—the orgasm crested and broke through her. Her back arched off the bed, her neck bowed and a long, keening howl issued from her throat.

Frantic, masculine hisses rasped into her ear. A gasp, a groan, a guttural growl, then he lost his breath—the telling absence of noise she'd been waiting for—which told her he'd found release as well.

Unable to help herself, Rowan smiled, waited for her labored, wholly satisfied breathing to return to normal. She didn't want to ruin the perfection of this moment with awkwardness, so she conjured a light laugh. "This girl," she gasped, still not completely recovered. "She's going to be one lucky lady."

Thankfully, Will read the tone correctly and played along. He chuckled. "So's your guy. I'll keep my fingers crossed that he lives up to your expectations."

It was Rowan's turn to laugh. *Now he had performance anxiety?* "Oh, I'm not worried about that," she replied confidently. "I'm certain he'll surpass my expectations. I hope your girl does the same."

A beat slid into three. "She already has," he murmured softly. "But I'll let you know how it goes."

"Good." The compliment warmed her, made her heart inexplicably swell with delight. She struggled to find her way out of the foggy realm of release. "Call me again, anytime."

"You can count on it."

"Goodnight, Will."

"G'night, Rowan."

10

"I CAN'T BELIEVE you've lived here all your life and you've never had a burger from Grady's," Rowan told him, still apparently scandalized on his behalf. He held the door open for her, followed her inside and then snugged a finger at the small of her back while he waited for his eyes to adjust to the dim interior. The scent of sizzling grease, pool chalk and smoke hung in the air, and the occasional crack of a cue ball finding its mark punctuated the low buzz of conversation.

Rowan led him deeper into the room until she found an empty table toward the back. "Brace yourself," she warned with a teasing smile as she slid into a cracked vinyl chair. "You're about to have the culinary experience of your life."

Will grinned, took the chair opposite her. Apparently this was a week for firsts then. First phone sex. First pool hall burger. Made a guy wonder what could possibly come next.

He'd probably *come* next, Will thought with a

smothered snort. Had almost come again this morning when he'd picked her up. Last night had been... Well, there were simply no words for how last night had been, Will decided, because it had been completely out of the realm of his experience. One minute the wordplay had been teasing, the next he'd had his dick in his hand listening to Rowan's *genuine* cries of sexual bliss.

What had once seemed, quite honestly, like a pointless waste of time, or a pathetic option for the undersexed, suddenly held considerable appeal. In fact, though he was hardly an amateur in the bedroom, he could honestly admit that he'd never in his life experienced anything so...erotic.

Hearing those thrillingly graphic words come out of that lush, ripe mouth had literally hot-wired his groin. The air in his lungs had thinned, his mouth had watered, then parched, and he'd had one of the *biggest* hard-ons he'd ever had in his life. His lips quirked in wry amusement. It was enough to give a guy the big head—literally.

Naturally, he couldn't wait to do it again.

And with that in mind, he'd done a little pre-emptive groundwork this morning when he'd picked her up. Last night, things could have easily turned...awkward, but Rowan had taken care of that by making sure the conversation moved into lighter territory immediately afterward.

In order to avoid the same scenario this morning, the moment she'd opened the door, Will had stepped forward, framed her face and kissed her until he could breathe again—hell, he'd felt like a damned fish out of water since last night—kissed her until he knew beyond a shadow of a doubt that the instantaneous heat had burned up any misgivings or second thoughts she might have entertained.

He meant to continue as he intended to go on, and backtracking simply wasn't an option.

He wanted her. Had to have her. It was more than mere attraction, more than exaggerated sexual chemistry. It was as though she'd unwittingly tapped into a secret power supply. He felt energized, brighter, bigger and better when he was with her. Will let go a shaky breath.

Powerful stuff, that.

And this morning at Doris's had been no exception. Will loved his job, honestly loved what he did. He counted himself among the rare few who actually made a comfortable living doing something that constituted work, but in truth, didn't feel like it. Yes, he ran into the occasional problem— like Doris, he thought uncharitably—but by and large, the majority of his clients were amiable and easy to please, and when he finished a project, he was rarely dissatisfied.

But working side-by-side with Rowan today had

been a singularly pleasing treat. He couldn't say that he'd learned any particular character traits—he'd already deduced that she was a hard worker. Her garden alone had told him that. Just like it had told him that she was organized in her own bizarre way, observant and diligent. Still, watching her get in there today and literally get her hands dirty, watching the expedient way her mind worked had jazzed him in a way that defied explanation.

While he had several teams of employees, this was the first time in his professional life that he'd felt like a part of one. It was her, he knew. Something about her just did it for him. She'd unwittingly injected something into his life that he hadn't realized he'd been missing—excitement.

Will leaned back in his chair and took a moment to simply look at her. Her long brown hair had been twisted into a thick braid which curved like a provocative question mark around one generous breast. Those gorgeous green eyes—which seemed startlingly bright against her healthy tan—were framed with thick curling lashes a shade lighter than her hair. Half a dozen freckles dusted her dainty nose and he'd noted a dimple in her left cheek this morning which had previously escaped his notice. He didn't know how he'd missed it since he spent so much time staring at that lush mouth, but it had nonetheless come as quite a shock when the adorable indentation had flashed at him this morning. Will sighed, momentarily lost in the sheer perfection of her face.

There were a million little things that made her beautiful. The sweet curve of her cheek, the smooth arc of her brow, even the delicate skin at her temple. He knew she'd undoubtedly look at herself and find flaws—women typically did, being women—but if she could see herself the way he did… Well, there'd simply be no question.

A slow smile moved across her lips as she suddenly caught him staring. Will blinked, felt his mouth slide into a sheepish grin. "Sorry," he apologized. "I just—" He shrugged, expelled a helpless breath. *Lay it all out on the line,* he thought. It seemed to be working so far. He lowered his voice. "You're beautiful."

Something warm shifted in her twinkling gaze. "Thank you," she murmured. He felt her gaze trace the planes of his face, felt it linger over his lips. "You're not too hard to look at yourself."

A waitress arrived, sparing him an immediate reply. Once she'd moved away, Will found his voice once more. "So how do you think things are going?" he asked. "Are you pleased with the way things are moving along?"

Rowan nodded. "Yeah, I am. You've got a great crew."

Will kicked his chair back, tilting the front legs off the floor. "It makes all the difference in the world, believe me."

"I would imagine so." She leaned back as their drinks arrived. "Doris seems okay with everything so far. What's your take on her?"

"She's happy." He shrugged lightly, grinned. "And like I told you before, she's connected. I wouldn't be at all surprised if you didn't end up being my competition."

Rowan crossed her arms and rested them on the table. She shot him a wry look. "I seriously doubt that."

"I don't," Will told her, and he meant it. She was seriously talented. "You've got an excellent eye and you know what you're doing. That and a little determination is all it takes."

"Yeah, well, I might consider it once I finish paying for my *first* education," she replied drolly.

"Ah," Will sighed knowingly. "Student loans, the bane of every self-made young professional."

She quirked a brow. "Is that the voice of experience?"

Will bit the inside of his cheek. "Er…no."

She leaned back in her seat and chuckled knowingly. "So which sports scholarship did you land? Wait. No. Let me guess." Her appraising gaze did another thorough inspection and he had the pleasure of watching admiration light a sparkler of desire in those leaf-green orbs. "You've got the lean, athletic look of a baseball player, but given your temper and wit, my money's on football, quarterback. Am I right?"

Will chuckled, impressed. "Yes, you're right."

She laughed and smacked her hand against the tabletop. "I knew it."

"You're good, I'll give you that. I think maybe you're in the wrong profession. Perhaps you should have been a detective."

"Nah." She shook her head. "I don't have the patience."

Will chased a bead of condensation down the side of his drink with his thumb. "What about teaching? Do you like it?"

She barely hesitated, but he felt it all the same. "Er…yeah, I do. I do," she repeated, and he got the distinct impression that she was trying to convince herself as much as him. Her gaze slid to his, and she winced. "Honestly, I'd much rather be outside doing what we did today, but hindsight's twenty-twenty." She pulled a shrug. "The fact is I've got a degree that I haven't finished paying for yet, and I'm too practical to give it up simply because it isn't as satisfying as I thought it would be."

Well, Will certainly understood that. Still…

"Not one of those proponents of the life's-too-short argument?" Will asked lightly.

A self-deprecating smile tugged at the corner of her distracting mouth. "In theory, yes. In practice, no."

Once again the idea of putting her to work for him on a permanent basis crossed his mind. Will instinctively knew she'd be a good choice, a fantastic addition. But if he made the offer now, he was afraid she'd suspect his motives. Better to wait until she'd finished Doris's project, then he could cite her excellent performance. Another thought struck, and though he knew it was none of his business, he simply had to ask. "What about your 900-line?" Will asked lightly. "You probably won't have a lot of time for it anymore, right?"

Rowan shot him a slightly frozen look, then sighed happily as their waitress returned once more, this time with a tray laden with food. She completely ignored his question, which wasn't the least bit encouraging. Will resisted the urge to swear. Why couldn't he leave well enough alone? he wondered. Last night he'd called her after she'd just gotten home, and today he was quizzing her about *her* business, which incidentally had nothing to do with him. Still, he couldn't help it. He didn't want her having phone sex with anyone but him. Selfish? Unrealistic? Yes, but he didn't care.

The idea of her talking to another guy the way that she'd talked to him—even pretending—set his teeth on edge and made a red haze swim in front of his eyes.

"Get ready," she warned with a playful smile. "I'm about to change your life."

Will barely swallowed an ironic chuckle. He had a sneaking suspicion she already had. He conjured a laugh all the same, easily caught up in her enthusiasm. "If you say so," he offered skeptically.

Actually, it smelled really good. Quite frankly, he hadn't been the least bit hungry when he'd suggested that they break for lunch—he'd just wanted a reason to be alone with her. Self-serving? Yes. But he didn't care. And evidently she was hungry, so no harm no foul, right?

"Well," Rowan prodded impatiently. "Go ahead."

Will blinked. "Oh, sorry." He glanced at her untouched plate. "What? Are you waiting on me?"

"Yes," she said, heaving a protracted sigh.

"Okay." Will feigned appropriate chagrin, and quickly took up his burger. One bite validated her reverence. His eyes widened in delight as his taste buds experienced what he could only liken to an orgasm. His astonished gaze flew to hers and he made a low growl of appreciation. "It's great," he moaned thickly.

She nodded approvingly and a smug grin drifted over her lips. "I told you so," she said pointedly, a direct dig at his own lamentable tendency to toot his own horn.

Will smiled, wiped the corner of his mouth. "Touché."

For a moment they ate in companionable silence, content to simply enjoy their food.

Then Will made the mistake of looking up.

Rowan's tongue darted out and licked the smear of ketchup from the corner of her mouth.

For all intents and purposes, she might as well have licked his rod.

Without warning that suffocating feeling blindsided him again, and in an instant, he was hard. Not semiaroused, or mildly turned-on—granite-*hard*.

The din around them faded into insignificance, and he wanted her so desperately that he honestly thought his reason might completely snap and he'd make the monumental error of devouring her right now—in public—the way he'd told her he wanted to last night.

She caught him staring once more. The tentative smile she wore faded and he had the pleasure of watching those leaf-green eyes darken into a somnolent mossy shade. Her lids drooped, presumably under the weight of desire, and whether the move was intentional or not, Will couldn't say, but that facile tongue—the very one that had locked his loins in a fiery pit of hell—peeked out once more, glided slowly over that ripe bottom lip. His dick actually strained toward her, as though she were one of Satan's angels, and it her devoted familiar.

She let go a soft shuddering breath, swallowed, then quietly excused herself to the bathroom. Once she was out of earshot, Will squeezed his eyes tightly shut and uttered a sizzling, succinct oath. He rubbed the bridge of his nose with curiously shaky fingers and made a valiant effort to get himself under control while she was gone. Sheesh. He had to get a grip. He simply had to—

His cell chirped and, with an annoyed grunt, he unsnapped it from his waist. He glanced at the Caller ID display, but didn't recognize the number. "Hello."

"You can't look at me like that, Will, especially in public. It…does things to me."

Rowan? Confused, Will blinked, darted a look over his shoulder. His heart rate kicked into overdrive. "I'm…sorry?" Will replied, uncertain as to what she expected him to say.

"You should be," she murmured, her voice a low throaty purr that instantly hissed through his blood. Impossibly, he hardened even more. "When you look at me like that—like you want to eat me up, *devour* me—my joy juice starts flowing and I get an itch that I can't scratch. It's…provoking."

Will grinned, darted a look around the crowded diner, then lowered his voice. "Yeah, well, watching you lick your lips is particularly provoking, too. In fact, you almost wound up with your burger in your lap. I came within a gnat's ass of upending the table."

A stuttered sigh sounded over the line, and when she spoke, her voice was distinctly thready. "Are you telling me that you've got a hard-on? Right now? Right this very minute?" More Rowan, less sex kitten. Utterly impossible to resist. Though he'd never in his life done anything remotely close to what he was about to do—have sex in a public place, a friggin' pool hall, no less—Will quietly stood, then started to make his way toward the bathroom.

"Baby, that's exactly what I'm saying." He chuckled lazily, past caring about control or anything else for that matter. He just wanted her. Had to have her. Right now. "I'm cocked, locked and ready to rock."

A beat slid to three and he listened to the thin, unsteady rasp of her breathing. "I *think* you should come back here."

Will rapped lightly on the door and a startled gasp sounded in his ear. He smiled. "I *think* you should open the door."

A THRILLING TORNADO of anticipation whirled through Rowan's abdomen and her gaze flew to the door. She barely resisted the urge to squeal with delight. It was crazy, what they were about to do. Scandalous, even, and instead of reprimanding herself for being out of control—for being reckless—she simply rode the rush of adrenaline rocketing through her bloodstream, gloried in the efficient way it heightened the need winding through her at warp-speed.

This was inevitable, she knew. Had been from the first moment she'd laid eyes on him. Last night had simply been a precursor, a wicked prelude to the grand event. This morning, she'd opened her door and before her mouth had even shaped the word "hello" he'd kissed her so thoroughly that she'd forgotten that she was tired, that she worried about being *weird* around him after the previous night, forgotten everything outside the feel of his lips against hers and the need blistering her veins.

She'd spent the entire day fantasizing about him—about a repeat performance of phone sex, then real sex, and every other sensually depraved scenario she could possibly dream up—had felt his presence, his sheer masculinity, pinging her like sonar all morning long. She'd been a complete wreck, a sexually deprived, single-minded *wreck* and nothing short of feeling him lodged deeply between her legs was going to cure what ailed her.

When she'd looked up a moment ago and caught him staring at her mouth again, saw those honey-brown eyes go heavy-lidded with smoky arousal, she'd absolutely lost it. So she'd calmly excused herself, then hid behind her phone to tell him what he'd done to her, never really intending to let things move to this point. Quite honestly, she simply wanted to torment him the way he'd tormented her

But then he'd told her about his hard-on—that part of him she craved so very desperately—and uttered that loaded *cocked, locked and ready to rock* phrase, and…she'd snapped. She'd wanted to teach him a lesson, and as it turned out, she was about to get one.

She wanted him now. Not later this afternoon, or even later tonight.

Now.

Rowan opened the door, and Will quickly strode in, seemingly without the smallest regard for the fact that he'd just entered the ladies' restroom. That they were about to do it in a pool hall/burger joint. How sexy was that? she thought, secretly elated. He shut the door, locked it with a purposeful click. Those honey eyes tangled with hers, effectively snatching the breath from her lungs, and the next second Rowan launched herself at him.

With a guttural growl of approval, Will matched her enthusiasm, crushed her to him and she actually whimpered he felt so good. His kiss was hot and frantic, thrilling and impatient, *thank God,* because though she'd undoubtedly relish every single minute of a grand seduction, she simply couldn't wait that long.

With every skilled thrust of his tongue into her mouth, she heard *Now! Now! Now!* An impressive bulge nudged her belly, branded her, and her lips slid into a grateful smile. *Cocked, locked and ready to rock,* indeed Rowan thought dimly as another rush of warmth coated her folds. She clenched her feminine muscles in a vain attempt to stem the flow, but she might as well have been trying to dam the Mississippi with a kitchen sponge—it wasn't gonna happen.

He tore his mouth from hers, then trailed thorough but speedy kisses down the side of her neck, along her jaw. Rowan untangled her fingers from his hair, eagerly jerked his shirt from the waistband of his shorts, then sighed with pleasure when her hands found his bare skin.

Warm, supple and smooth.

Sweet.

A low masculine hum of pleasure hissed out of him, and his belly shuddered gratifyingly beneath her fingers. Getting beneath the shirt wasn't enough—she wanted it off. She tugged the garment over his head, then slung it over the stall door. With a soft wicked chuckle, Will grasp the hem of her tank and swiftly drew it off as well. His hot gaze fastened on her chest and she had the pleasure of watching his eyes darken further. An unsteady breath puffed past his lips as he traced the lacy edge of her bra with slightly shaking fingers.

"It clasps in the front," Rowan told him, just in case he hadn't noticed.

"How fortuitous," he murmured thickly. He slipped his fingers beneath the fastener and gave it a gentle pop. The cups sagged, baring her taut nipples to his hungry gaze. Will let go a thin breath, lifted her from the waist, and gently set her down on the vanity. Then he bent his gorgeous head and fastened his greedy mouth onto her aching peak, expertly palming the other, lest it feel neglected.

Rowan gasped with pleasure and sagged beneath the weight of the exquisite torment. He suckled, kissed, licked and ravished. His tongue blazed a trail from peak to peak, alternately around each globe, then pulled each in turn deep into his hot mouth. A steady throb built between her legs, that itchy sensation intensified deep in her womb and she hooked her legs around his thighs, trying desperately to find some sort of relief. She wanted that weighty pressure, wanted desperately to feel that hard part of him between her legs. At this point she was shameless, wasn't too proud to beg.

She reached out and scored his muscled chest—his nipples—with her nails, leaned forward and nipped his powerful shoulder, then licked the hurt away, savored the salty essence of his skin. His scent invaded her nostrils, drugged her to the point of delirium, and simply shattering into a million little pieces if he didn't finish this soon became a genuine fear.

She squirmed closer to him, let her hand drift over his belly, then boldly stroked his groin. A hot thrill snaked through her at the intimate contact. He was gloriously hard, electrifyingly huge. She slipped the button of his shorts from its closure, then felt his warm breath hiss over her nipple as she lowered his zipper. An instant later, she had him in hand, tenderly working the hot, slippery flesh over his rigid length. She ran the pad of her thumb over his wet tip, then painted his engorged head with the evidence of his desire. Will jerked, shuddered, beneath her ministrations, and a low growl of warning issued from his throat.

She felt his warm fingers against her belly, felt her shorts give way beneath his questing hands. His mouth found hers once more.

A hot probing kiss, the dizzying rasp of his tongue against hers.

She alternately lifted her hips as he tugged her shorts and panties down in agonizingly slow increments. She watched, mesmerized, as Will withdrew a condom from his wallet, then his shorts and briefs sagged to his knees and he efficiently rolled the protection into place.

She blinked drunkenly, astonished at his sheer size, and another thick warm rush of heat seeped into her weeping folds. Her nipples tingled and the air in her lungs virtually evaporated. Her neck suddenly felt too weak to support her head, and anticipation made her belly tremble violently.

Will grasped her hips, scooted her forward, then guided himself to her center. The first nudge of him between her nether lips made Rowan inhale sharply—then he smoothly slid inside her, buried every glorious inch of himself to the hilt—and she exhaled in sublime, wondrous satisfaction. The storm inside her briefly abated, seemingly in awe of the flawless perfection of this moment. It didn't matter that they were hiding in a bathroom, that her panties hung from one ankle, or that, on the other side of the door, roughly fifty unsuspecting people sat calmly eating their lunch.

Nothing mattered but him being inside her— *finally.*

Her world shifted and she clung to him, resisted the curious urge to weep. *Home, sweet home,* she thought. For no particular reason, she tried to tell herself. But she knew better. Knew that she'd never be the same.

Will expelled a harsh breath and he rested his forehead against hers, locked himself inside her. His hands came up and gently framed her face, then with a tender heart-wrenchingly sweet look, he lowered his mouth to hers once more.

One moment of tenderness in a maelstrom of mindlessness was all it took for her silly heart to melt like a pat of butter over a hot bun.

A curiously relieved laugh stuttered out of her mouth. She looped her arms around his neck, threw every ounce of passion she possessed into the kiss and simultaneously clamped her greedy muscles around him. Pleasure barbed through her, and the single wanton act was all it took to make Will forget about being tender. His palms slid down her sides, grazed the margins of her breasts, then wound around until her bottom rested in his hands. He kneaded her rump as he slid in and out of her, a hot thrilling game of seek and retreat that quickly stoked the fire raging through her blood.

A coil of tingly heat tightened in her womb and her breathing came in sharp little puffs as he upped the tempo.

Harder, faster, then harder still.

Will's breathing grew labored as well, and a

fine dew of sweat glistened on his shoulders. He pumped in and out of her, a rhythmic, erotic bump and grind that made her nipples quiver and dance as a result of his frantic, manic thrusts.

Rowan couldn't get enough of him. Her hands mapped his body. His shoulders, his belly, the small of his back and, when the first sparker of beginning release detonated in her womb, she anchored them on his ass and writhed wildly against him.

Will growled low in his throat, a masculine sound of pleasure that sang in her veins.

"Will," Rowan gasped brokenly. "I need— I'm almost—"

Will increased his rhythm, pounded into her. One hand left her bottom, came around and massaged her clit. The shock of sensation rent a soundless wail from the back of her throat, and a few clever strokes later she came so hard she honestly feared she might lose consciousness. Her vision blackened around the edges, colors faded into gray, and if he hadn't held her upright, she would have undoubtedly melted into the floor.

Wave after wave of release eddied through her, sucking her under, lifting her up. Heightened sensation bolted through her with every eager spasm of the orgasm.

She heard Will's breath catch in his throat, felt him tense, then a low keening growl sounded next to her ear as three hard thrusts later, he joined her in paradise. A shock of warmth pooled against the back of her womb, sending another tingle of joy through her.

To her unreasonable delight, Will didn't immediately withdraw from her, but rather lingered between her legs. A guy too quick on the dismount was a pet peeve of hers, and she was secretly thrilled that he wasn't going to be guilty of that offense.

He braced one palm on the vanity, then tipped her chin up. His eyes sparkled with latent humor and lingering lust, and just a smidge of something else. Affection, maybe? "That was spectacular," Will murmured warmly, caressing each word with meaningful intent.

Rowan smiled. "I agree."

"Do you have plans for tonight?"

Her smile widened and hesitant joy expanded in her chest. "No," she said slowly.

Will's gaze traced the curves of her face, dropped and lingered on her lips. "Then come be with me. I want to devour you...more slowly... next time."

Mama mia. Rowan barely suppressed a shiver. She nodded, unable to form a coherent reply.

Ever so slowly, he pulled out of her, and she swallowed a wince of regret, already missing his warmth.

A sharp rap on the door interrupted her mini-pity party and her alarmed gaze flew to Will's equally shocked expression. She almost choked on a laugh.

Rowan scrambled from the vanity while Will disappeared behind the stall, presumably to remove the condom. A flush of the commode confirmed her assessment. She snagged a paper towel from the rack on the wall and quickly did a little damage control as well. "Er…someone's in here," she called loudly.

Silence, then, "Rowan, is that you?"

Rowan froze in the process of tugging her panties back up her legs. *Alexa?* She looked up and caught Will's questioning look. "It's my friend," she said quietly. "Yeah," she admitted in slightly carrying tones. She shoved her legs back into her shorts and swiftly pulled them up. "I'll, uh… I'll be out in a minute." Well, this was just great. She'd wanted Alexa to meet Will, but these were hardly ideal circumstances. Her friend, she knew, would roast her mercilessly.

"Get the lead out, would you? You've been in there *forever.* I've got to pee like a Russian racehorse and some old geezer is holed up in the men's room."

Rowan refastened her bra, snagged her shirt then dragged it over her head. She rolled her eyes. "Sorry," she called, exasperated.

"Will!"

Holy shit, Rowan thought, jumping almost out of her skin. Will's mother again. What the hell was with the screaming? she wondered.

Will jerked, startled as well and swore hotly, then patted his shorts down until he found his phone. "I'll call you back, Mom," Will growled, then cut the power to prevent her from saying anything else.

But it was too late. Though she couldn't see Alexa's face, Rowan knew beyond a shadow of a doubt that she'd heard Will's mother—hell, she wouldn't be surprised if everyone in the damned restaurant had heard her.

Sure enough, Alexa's loaded voice sounded through the door. *"Will?"* she asked, her voice rife with happy innuendo. "Rowan, why do I get the feeling that you're not alone?"

Will and Rowan shared a fatalistic look. Oh, well, Rowan thought. It wasn't like she was going to be able to walk out of the bathroom *alone.* She was busted, and truth be told, she'd rather be busted by Alexa than anyone else. She waited for Will to tuck in his shirt, then opened the door to find her friend on the other side. Alexa's twinkling, knowing gaze bounced back and forth between them and she grinned widely.

"It's your third eye," Rowan deadpanned. "I guess it's not blind after all."

"Does that mean my other prediction came true as well?" Alexa asked, her voice a study in mystery.

From the corner of her eye she watched Will's forehead wrinkle with perplexity. Rowan felt her lips twitch, rocked back on her heels. "It certainly did."

Alexa whooped delightedly, shot Will an admiring look. She considered him for a wistful moment, then her mysterious gaze found Rowan's once more. "I just made another prediction," she said softly. "Wanna hear it?"

Not in mixed company, she was sure, Rowan thought, suddenly nervous. Her stomach did a little roll. She had a grim suspicion she knew what her friend *predicted* and she wasn't ready to hear it yet, and most definitely not in front of Will.

Rowan shook her head. "I, uh... I think it'll keep."

Alexa lifted one shoulder in an innocent shrug. "Okay." She glanced at Will, then smiled and leaned forward to whisper in Rowan's ear. "Your shirt's on backward. I doubt anyone will notice that. But you might want to tell Will to close the barn door before you walk back into the dining room. *That,* as I'm sure you know, is *noticeable.*"

Unable to help herself, Rowan chuckled. Alexa disappeared into the bathroom, leaving them alone in the small hall.

"What?" Will asked. "What's so funny?"

Rowan moved in front of him, pressed him up against the wall with her body. A low hum of masculine pleasure vibrated up his throat as her hands went to the front of his shorts. She leaned forward and kissed him, ate his startled wince as she closed his zipper with a quick, telling jerk.

Rowan laughed as his mortification sunk in. He thunked his head back against the wall and swore. "Christ."

"Don't sweat it," she chuckled. "She was impressed."

"And that's supposed to make me feel better?" He passed a hand over his adorably red face.

Rowan sidled closer to him once more, lowered her voice. "Would it help to know that *I* was impressed?"

He stilled, seemingly mollified. "You were?"

"And I'm looking forward to being impressed again," she told him, leaning forward to nip at his bottom lip. Lust kindled again. "What time did you want me to come over?"

He settled his hands on her waist, doodled his thumbs on her sides. "As soon as you can."

"I'll be there," she murmured. Another wicked thrill wound through her.

And she couldn't wait.

11

"I DON'T LIKE being hung up on, William," his mother chastised. "It's rude."

"I didn't mean to hang up on you, Mom. I hit a dead spot." Will shut down his computer and tidied his desk, made sure that everything was taken care of before he called it a day. For the first time in years, he was leaving early.

"At Grady's Pool Hall?" she asked incredulously. "It's less than a mile from here."

Will pulled an offhand shrug. "It happens."

She snorted indelicately, pushed off from the door frame. "Indeed it might, but that's not what happened when I called you, and I know it. If you were on a date and didn't want to talk to me, then just say so. Don't tell me you hit a dead spot."

Will glanced up. "Who said anything about being on a date?"

Her eyebrows shot up. "Well, weren't you? The whole crew was abuzz about your *extended* lunch break with the woman you've found to handle Doris's design. A woman I have yet to meet, by the way," she added pointedly, "and to my knowledge, you've never hired a single soul without getting my input first." She drew herself up. "I know that technically I'm just your secretary, Will, but I always thought…" She left the rest unsaid, waiting for the guilt to settle on his shoulders. "Ah, well. An old woman's folly, I suppose."

Oh, shit, Will thought shifting uncomfortably. He should have anticipated this. He'd avoided the Rowan issue with his mother because, quite frankly, she knew him too well. He knew the instant she saw him with Rowan—or even heard him talk about Rowan, for that matter—the cat would be out of the bed, so to speak, and she'd start planning a guest list for a fall wedding.

Will blew out a breath, rubbed the back of his neck. "Mom, you know that you're not just my secretary. I didn't get your input on this one because there simply wasn't time." He cited Doris's impending guests and shot her a helpless look. "I stumbled into this solution and took advantage of it. End of story. If you want to meet her, come by Doris's."

She was mollified entirely too quickly for Will's comfort and her gaze turned shrewd. "Rumor has it if I wanted to meet her sooner I could come to your house tonight."

Will stifled the urge to grind his teeth. He didn't know which one of those jack-legged bastards had told her that, but come tomorrow morning, someone's ass was his. Still, when faced with an outright question, he found it too difficult to lie. "That's true."

She beamed at him. "So lunch was really a date?" she pressed like a dog with a soup bone.

Will smothered a snort, remembering those wonderful, frantic minutes in the bathroom. In the friggin' bathroom. He'd never lost control like that. Had never been swept up in an attraction so fierce that he couldn't contain himself. But he had with her. His blood heated at the mere thought and an impatient twang strummed across his nerves. "You could call it that, yes."

She sighed, evidently pleased. "Excellent. From what I hear, you and she have a lot in common."

Who the hell was running their mouth? Will wondered, irritated. Wasn't a guy allowed to have any secrets?

"Where did you meet her again?" she queried lightly. Too lightly. "I don't believe I've heard you say."

Speaking of secrets, Will thought, with a mental shudder. That was one he planned to take to his grave. He could just hear himself. *Remember that phone sex operator that Scott called, Mom?*

Well, she might just be the mother of your future grandchildren.

Will stilled. Future grandchildren? he thought, suddenly shaken. A queasy feeling swelled in his gut. He'd, uh… He'd sort of made a leap there, hadn't he? One session of spectacular phone sex and a lengthy lunch holed up in the bathroom in a local pool hall having mind-blowing, soul-shattering sex did not a future wife make. Right?

Right.

Was he protesting too much? He didn't think so, and just to prove it he allowed the image of Rowan decked out in a long white gown with a garland of fresh flowers crowning that waist-length mink-colored hair to materialize in his head. The picture made his heart leap and a whirling sensation spin behind his navel. He told himself it was nausea, though he grimly suspected it might be another emotion altogether, one he wasn't anywhere near ready to explore.

Another image surfaced, a snapshot into his fictional future. In this one, she held a chubby-cheeked little girl with brown hair, leafy eyes, dimpled legs and bare feet. His upper lip grew moist.

"Son?"

Will blinked, jerked from the fantasy. "Yeah?"

"Where did you meet her?"

"Er…a mutual friend." He supposed he could call Scott a friend. Splitting hairs, he knew, but he wasn't about to tell her the truth. He'd given Rowan his word that he wouldn't share her secret, and though his mother clearly didn't believe him—and clearly didn't appreciate it—that promise extended to her as well. "Okay," he sighed resolutely. "I'm out of here."

"Out of here? B-b-but it's only f-f-four o'clock," she sputtered, whirling around as he strode past.

"I know," Will replied with exaggerated patience. "I learned how to tell time in first grade." He flashed her a smile. "Bye, Mom. I've got a date." With that parting comment, he headed for his truck.

Before he'd left Doris's this afternoon, he'd asked Rowan to bring her bathing suit and a bottle of her favorite wine, and he'd take care of the rest. Therefore a swift trip to the grocery store was in order, thus his excuse for leaving early. He also intended to get his dirty clothes out of his pantry. The thought drew a smile.

Which brought to mind *her* smile.

Which brought to mind *her* lips.

Which brought to mind *her* kiss.

Which brought to mind sex…with *her.*

Honestly, it was a vicious cycle, Will thought as a vision of her bare breasts and dewy curls leaped obligingly to mind. Tight nipples, the gentle swell of her belly, the perfect curve of her hip, and those tanned thighs wrapped around him, pulling him deeper and deeper into her heat. He let go a shaky breath.

Will had been turned on before, he'd even had great sex. But never in his life had he experienced anything remotely close to the chemistry and heat—the sheer perfection—of being with Rowan Crosswhite. When he'd finally pushed himself between her legs, he'd filled his lungs with more oxygen than they'd ever held—then she'd clenched around him and he'd promptly lost it again.

It had been the strangest sensation. The hair on the back of his neck had prickled, a hum of electricity had raced up his spine, then radiated out over his shoulders, buzzed down his arms and tingled into his fingertips.

The moment had been too rife with some unnamed something to merely let it pass, so he'd drawn her to him and kissed her again…and then he'd been lost. Lost in her sighs and kisses, lost in her heat, lost in a world where the only thing that mattered was being with her—being *inside* her.

He wanted that mindlessness again, Will thought, swallowing as a curious sensation commenced in his chest. Today had merely been an appetizer—tonight he fully intended to devour her.

Every freckle, every mole, every white part, every pink part. He smiled in anticipation.

All her parts.

ROWAN FISHED her cell phone out of her purse, then punched in Will's number and waited for him to pick up. Her heart skipped a beat at the sound of his voice. "Hello."

"Hey," she said warmly. "Just wanted to let you know I'm on my way. I'm, uh, running a little late." She shifted into fourth gear, nudged the horses into action, and the purr of the motor had its usual calming effect.

"What happened?"

Rowan rolled her eyes, strummed her fingers on the steering wheel. "*Ida* happened."

His sexy chuckle sounded in her ear. "Let me guess. Another errand?"

"Her new orthopedic shoes came in today. I had to go get them for her."

"Well, look at this way." Though he was trying to be helpful, she could hear the humor in his voice. "At least it wasn't another enema or wart remover."

"In the morning I have to wax her upper lip," she said flatly.

A shocked laugh burst from his throat. "I hesitate to point this out, but she could have asked for a Brazilian, then you would have really been in trouble."

"Too true," Rowan conceded with a laugh, equally relieved and revolted. Though she grumbled, she truly didn't mind running errands for Ida. It gave her something to do to fill up her day, to keep her from thinking about being alone or cast adrift. She turned onto his road, and breathed a curious sigh of relief. Almost there. With him. Where she instinctively knew things would instantly get better.

"Where are you?" Will asked.

"A couple of miles from your house."

"Good," he murmured suggestively, "then we've got time for a quickie. Wanna hear something cool that happened to me today?"

Rowan felt a smile drift around her lips and a secret thrill whipped through her. She'd created a monster. Hell, she was game if he was. She liked shocking him, hearing those wicked words come out of those sexy lips.

In fact, playing the part of the naughty phone sex operator last night had been particularly hard, especially after her *stimulating* conversation with Will, and she grimly suspected it was only going to get harder. But she really needed the money, and it seemed impractical to quit just because she didn't enjoy it. Hell, she'd never enjoyed it. So why should now be any different?

She knew the difference—Will had made the difference. He'd showed her what she'd been missing, which made it all the more difficult to pretend.

Furthermore, he'd made that leading little comment about her not having time for her 1-900-line anymore, and the only thing which had saved her from an awkward reply had been the timely arrival of their waitress.

Rowan knew that now that she'd gone to work for him, that he fully expected her to give up the 1-900-line. Considering that she'd cited immediate money woes and those woes were now basically nonexistent, it wasn't an illogical deduction. But just because she didn't need the money right now didn't mean that she wouldn't need it in the future. It just wasn't practical. Regrettably, she had more to consider than Will Foster's pride.

Rowan dragged her thoughts back to the conversation at hand. "Sure. What happened to you today?"

"That girl I told you about last night? We had an…interesting lunch date."

Rowan bit the corner of her lip, remembering. Warmth rushed to her core. "Oh? What did you do?"

"We had wild, mindless sex in the ladies' bathroom of a local pool hall." His voice held a strangled quality.

She let go a shuddering breath, felt the tips of

her breasts tingle with remembered heat. "Sounds fun. Did you like it?"

A short burst of laughter sounded in her ear. "I more than liked it. I loved it. She rocked my world. She has the most amazing little body. Everything is tight and compact. Her breasts are a mere nod away from my mouth," he murmured, seemingly distracted. "Did I tell you that I tasted them? That the feel of her taut nipple on my tongue made me almost *explode?* That it took every ounce of will-power I owned to take care of her first, to make sure that she came. I didn't want her to think I was a lazy lover," he added.

Rowan swallowed an ironic snort. "I seriously doubt that was ever in question." There was nothing remotely lazy about Will Foster.

"Sliding into her, feeling her greedy body clenching around me was the single most amazing sensation I've ever had. Hell, we were in a bathroom—*a bathroom, dammit!*—with a roomful of people on the other side of the door, and I swear, the building could have tumbled down around me and I—" He sighed. "I wouldn't have blinked. I was too caught up in her. Lost in her."

Rowan let go a soft sigh, felt her goofy heart swell as she listened to him talk about their afternoon. About being with her. "She sounds like a lucky girl."

He chuckled, lightening the curiously tense moment. "I would hope she'd agree."

"I'm sure she would," Rowan said drolly. "Would you like to hear about my day?"

Another sexy laugh, then, "Would I ever."

"Remember that guy I told you about last night?" she murmured softly. "The one who makes me so hot my panties stay drenched when I'm around him?"

"Yes," he replied in a strangled voice. "I r-re-member."

"This afternoon, he and I made it in a bathroom as well. *It was fantastic,*" she moaned appreciatively. "One minute I was sitting there calmly eating my lunch. Then I caught him looking at my mouth—looking at me as though I was the last loaf of bread on the shelf before a winter storm—and I… I just snapped. I mean, the nerve of this guy! How could he sit there and look at me like that? Literally light me up—in public, no less—and then not do anything about it? How could he just sit there and expect me to eat my burger, when I wanted to *eat* him, or better yet have him eat *me*." Rowan let go a sigh, pressed her thighs together to stem the flow of heat gathering at her center. "So I did what any pathetically horny girl would do—I excused myself into the bathroom, then I called him, and I called his sexy ass on the carpet."

"That bastard," Will teased unsteadily. "I hope you gave him what he deserved."

"Oh, no. I've just gotten started with this guy. I'm thinking some serious torture sessions are due. I want to blow him until he weeps, then ride him until he his eyes roll back in his head. I want to make him beg," she all but growled. She was so hot she could barely drive, but pulling over would only delay being with him. She couldn't bear it.

Geez, God, she did want to do all these things to him, but she honestly couldn't believe she had the nerve to say them. Would have never believed that she would say those things to a guy and mean them and, even though a part of her insisted on making him lose it as well, Rowan knew that her desire to keep the upper hand only played a small part in why she could let go with him. Why she could say the things she said. For whatever reason, she felt safe with him. Felt the chaos of her world hit a lull and she clung to the hope of that feeling.

Will swallowed audibly. "Make him pay, baby, that's all I can say. Make him pay."

Rowan grinned, swung her car into his drive. She could hear the purr of her car from his end of the line, so she knew he had to have heard her as well.

She pulled around to the back, saw Will standing next to the grill, his barbecue tongs forgotten in his hand. He looked at her and smiled, a grin that was at once hot, happy and a wee bit stunned. She liked that, Rowan decided. Liked that she'd shocked him.

He was barefoot and shirtless, and from the damp, slightly curly look of his hair, he'd either spent time in the shower or the pool, probably both, she decided. He'd slung a kitchen towel over his shoulder, and looked completely at home and unguarded. Relaxed. Need and affection broadsided her, pushing a wobbly smile into place.

She shifted into Park, killed the engine, then took off her sunglasses and grinned at him. "I'm here to collect."

He laughed, gestured toward the grill. "Can I have my last meal first?"

What? Hadn't she made that plain? Didn't she just tell him he could eat *her?* Rowan barely resisted the urge to tell him. Honestly, this scandalous behavior was coming a bit too easily to her for comfort.

She heaved an exaggerated long-suffering sigh, snagged the wine and climbed out of the car. "I suppose." She disconnected, then joined him by the grill and sniffed appreciatively. "Something smells good."

Will flipped the steaks over. "I picked up a couple of filets on my way home. How do you like yours?"

"Medium rare."

"Ah," he sighed. "A woman after my own heart."

"Is there anything I can do to help?"

"You could pour us a glass of wine." He nodded toward the table. "Glasses are over there, as well as a corkscrew."

Rowan grinned, arched a brow. "You're just a regular Boy Scout, aren't you?"

His honey gaze tangled with hers and a corner of his sexy mouth tucked into a grin. "Always prepared."

Well, he'd certainly prepared things this evening, Rowan thought, secretly pleased for all the trouble he'd apparently gone to on her behalf. He'd set a beautiful table, complete with candlelight, linen napkins and a bouquet of his prized roses. Honestly, she would have been just as happy with a paper plate and a Dixie cup, but this was unexpectedly...nice.

Will transferred the steaks onto a platter and brought them over to the table. "Okay. We're ready."

Rowan dressed her salad. "Thanks," she told him. "This looks wonderful."

"You know, I've been thinking," Will began in that too light tone that usually preceded an awkward conversation. "In light of how fast our relationship has progressed to an intimate level, I uh...really don't know that much about you."

She speared a tomato wedge and dragged it through her dressing, then popped it into her mouth. Rowan chewed thoughtfully, considered him. This was true, she decided. Though she honestly felt like she'd known him forever, other than his name, his profession, his respect for the past, for the soil and every hair, freckle and mole on his body, she really didn't know him at all. She resisted the urge to smile.

Rowan took her time swallowing. "What would you like to know?"

"I guess I could sit here and ask about family, friends, dreams, goals and desires—" Will smiled "—but what I really want to know is this—why aren't you married yet?"

She blinked. "Come again?"

Will exhaled a mighty breath. "You're wonderful," he explained. "You're smart, bright and funny. Sexy as hell," he added with an implied growl. "Why hasn't somebody snatched you up yet? I find it hard to believe no one's asked."

Flattered, Rowan felt the warmth of the compliment down to her little toes. She shot him a droll look. "Someone asked," she admitted.

"And you said no?"

"No," she sighed. "I stupidly said yes."

A puzzled line emerged between his brows

and he opened his mouth to ask the obvious question. "But—"

"I called it off."

"Because…" he prodded expectantly when she didn't elaborate.

God, this was so embarrassing. Logic told her that it hadn't been her fault that Mark had cheated, but there was still a small part of her that held on to insecurities, that held on to was-I-woman-enough? worries and all that baggage.

Rowan poked her tongue into her cheek and smiled ruefully. "Because I caught him in bed with another woman. Good enough reason, wouldn't you say?"

Will nodded, winced. "Yeah, I'd say so."

Rowan slouched back in her chair, took a sip of wine and waited for the alcohol to dull her senses. "Do you know what I really regret about all that mess?"

He shook his head, silently encouraging her.

Rowan's gaze slid to her car, felt her eyes narrow into little pissed-off slits. "I let that cheating bastard drive my car. My dad told me when he gave it to me that any guy that would *ask* to drive it wasn't worthy of my attention, to basically kick his ass to the curb."

"Sounds like good advice."

Rowan nodded. "I used that strategy with every

guy I dated—I *never* let any guy drive my car—
right up until Mark." She chuckled grimly. "He slid
right under my radar."

"It can happen," Will told her.

Rowan looked up, her senses going on point.
"Since we're sharing, is that the voice of experience?"

He worked a kink out of his shoulders and a dry
bark of laughter erupted from his throat. "Oh,
hell, yeah."

"What happened?"

His gaze drifted to hers, held it. "Same scenario, but we weren't engaged. She made a complete
fool of me."

"I find that hard to believe."

Will laughed without humor. "So do I, now."

Her gaze turned inward. "Why does it always
have to be so hard, I wonder? Finding the right person? Other people do it and make it look easy."

He hesitated. "I don't think it's ever easy."

"Okay," she qualified. "Maybe easy's not the
right word. But they make it work." She cast him
a glance, traced the smooth lines of his face and
felt a muddled heat stir in her loins. Her nipples
tingled and a bud of need bloomed in her belly. "Is
your mother right, Will?" she asked softly. "Are
you lonely?"

She was, though she was loath to admit it. For

all her independent-woman bravado, there were times when she thought if she spent another minute in her own company she'd scream. Most of the time she was content, but some secret source of information—intuition, maybe?—told her that being content now would never be good enough.

Not after Will Foster.

That sticky-honey gaze found hers and held. "Sometimes," he admitted. Then he leaned forward, bracketed her face with his big, warm hands, forcing a soft sigh from her mouth, and kissed her gently. "But not now," he whispered. "Not while I'm with you."

Her either, Rowan decided dimly.

Not right now.

And definitely not tonight.

12

NOT WHILE I'M WITH YOU.

Truer words had never been spoken, Will thought as he lowered his mouth to hers, felt her talented fingers slide into his hair. Right up until this very minute he would have denied that he was ever lonely, but the fact was, he'd been lonely all along and had been simply too stubborn or too blind—hell, most likely both—to see it.

Until Rowan, he'd had no frame of reference, no way to put the sentiment in context. The whole suffocating feeling, the fish-out-of-water panic—that had been his body's way of telling him what his mind already knew, which was, he'd be lonely without her.

He needed her.

Thankfully for Will, at the moment one need superseded another, blotted out complicated thoughts of feelings and fears.

He simply wanted to feel.

Wanted to feel her bare skin beneath his palms,

her greedy hands stroking his body. Wanted to take her to bed and love her properly.

He tore his mouth away from hers. "Let's go inside," he suggested softly.

She nodded wordlessly. Those gorgeous green eyes had darkened into a shade of mountain fern and glistened with desire so fierce and strong it was simply breathtaking. He laced his fingers through hers, led her silently through the house and into his bedroom.

She looked out his French doors into his rose garden and a knowing smile curled her lush lips, lightened the mood between them.

Will quirked a brow. "What?"

"I was right," she murmured.

"Right about what?"

"Your garden. I thought you'd be able to access it from your bedroom." She sighed wistfully. "It's even prettier from in here."

"You can say that again," Will told her, his voice inexplicably low.

He watched her lips curl into a droll smile and she sidled toward him. "Why do I get the feeling we're talking about two completely different things?"

"Because—and I think I've told you this before—you're very perceptive." He encircled her waist with his arms, smiled down at her, let his gaze purposely caress her lips. "In fact, I think that if you really put your mind to it you could divine what I'm thinking right now."

She laughed. "You mean have a psychic moment?"

He nodded. "Exactly."

Her gaze turned a smidge calculating and something about her wicked smile made him distinctly uneasy. She shrugged lightly. "I'll give it my best shot. I should probably touch something of yours if it's going to work properly." She leaned forward and licked the hollow of his throat, pulling a hiss from between his suddenly clenched teeth.

She smiled up at him, the she-devil, and a startled laugh broke up in his throat.

"Yeah, I think that helped," she told him. "I had a small vision." Her gaze drifted over his chest and she slipped her fingers into the waistband of his trunks. "But I should probably do it again just so that I can make sure I know what I'm talking about. I'd uh…hate to be accused of being a fraud."

She leaned forward and this time her talented tongue darted out and laved his nipple. Will winced and his dick jerked hard against her belly.

Another she-devil grin claimed her lips. "Yes, I think I definitely have a handle on it now."

He strangled on a laugh. He'd give her something to get a handle on, Will thought. He bent his head, found her mouth and then began to slowly propel her toward the bed. He kissed her hard and deep, slow and easy. God, he could kiss her forever, Will thought dimly. He slid his tongue along hers, pulled at it creating a delicious suction between their mouths, which he longed to mimic in their lower extremities.

The backs of her knees hit the edge of the mattress and, with a groan of delight, she sagged onto the bed. Will eagerly followed her down. He'd enjoyed every minute of the first time they'd made love. It had been hot and frantic, mindless and wanton. Fantastic. But he tended to be a little fastidious when it came to making love. He liked to nurture and tease, coax and coddle a bloom of release from a woman. Liked to take his time.

Rowan had blossomed for him this afternoon at the pool hall—*God had she ever*—but he suspected that she was like one of those rare night-blooming flowers and he couldn't wait to see her in all her glory.

He pulled away from her mouth, nuzzled her ear, then licked a slow path down the side of her neck. She shuddered beneath him, a wordless gesture of praise and he smiled against her. "You smell nice," Will murmured. "Like apples and daisies." Her belly shook as his fingers tugged at the hem of her shirt. "I wonder what you smell like here?" he asked, then bent his head and ran the tip of his tongue around the rim of her belly button. Gratifyingly, another shiver shook her.

Will nudged her shirt up farther, treated a couple of ribs to the same treatment. She whimpered, arched her back up off the bed, begging for a kiss of another sort. Will edged up her body, drew the garment over her head, cast it aside with a careless flick of his wrist, then let his gaze drift over her womanly frame. Soft mounds, feminine belly, dainty waist. His mouth parched, then watered. Her womanly scent invaded his nostrils, curled around his senses and suddenly, taking his time, plotting his next move like a road trip didn't seem quite so important.

He popped her bra open once more, then eagerly fastened his mouth upon her breast. Rowan arched again, pushing the tender globe further into his mouth. He hummed with pleasure, ate her up. Her hands were all over him—his back, his shoulders, in his hair. It was as though he'd tripped a secret button, one that sent her wild, and he found it inexplicably—incredibly—arousing. He sucked harder, trailed his fingers over her belly, then took advantage of the extra room beneath her waistband when another startled inhalation deflated her tummy.

She stilled, then squirmed when his fingers

brushed her curls. She gasped, then her own fingers made a determined trail to his shorts and she palmed him through the fabric, rubbed determinedly against him. "Oh, Will. I can't— I need— *Could you please hurry up?*"

He laughed. Moved to the other breast. Dragged a finger over her engorged clit. "Are we punching a time clock?"

"No," she growled, rocking suggestively beneath him. "But I'm burning up. You have to do something. I can't— I can't take it."

Will scooted down between her legs and dragged her shorts and panties over her hips. They joined her shirt and bra on the floor. He glanced at them and an evil little impulse took hold. He pretended to move away from her.

She propped herself up on her elbows. "Where are you going?" she asked incredulously.

"To put those in the dirty clothes hamper. I know how you hate laundry on the floor."

A stuttered laugh fizzed up her throat and her eyes widened in outrage. "Oh, you just wait." Her head sagged against the bed. "I am *so* going to get you."

Will chuckled. "Bring it on, badass," he goaded. "I'm ready whenever you are."

Her head popped back up and a martial glint suddenly sparked in her gaze. He realized at once that he'd made a mistake. He shouldn't have goaded her, shouldn't have teased her. But the power was simply intoxicating. It was the first time in his life he'd ever had this sort of control over a woman and he supposed he'd let it go to his head. It was an appalling abuse of his power, Will decided, and he should be ashamed. He grinned.

Should be...but he wasn't.

"Take those shorts off and we'll see who's the badass," Rowan told him.

He'd made a tactical error, but pride would not let him back down. Besides, he was perversely looking forward to this little game. He stood, shucked his trunks and kicked them aside. Her eyes dropped to his dick, she blinked slowly as though she'd had a little too much to drink, then she licked her lips.

"Come here." She fired the words at him like bullets, short and succinct, and he felt them lodge in his groin.

Will joined her on the bed. She sat up, rolled him onto his back then very determinedly began to lick him in the same thought-shattering, dick-provoking way he'd licked her. His nipples, his ribs, his belly button. Then—and though he'd been expecting it—looking forward to it, even—she still managed to pull a startled hiss from him when she took him in hand.

She worked him up and down, slowly, tenderly,

grazed the sides of his stiff shaft. "I've been think-ing about this all day," she told him, her voice foggy, sultry, that near-whisper that never failed to set him off. "Thinking about holding you, licking you—" she turned the thought into action, putting the entire length of his throbbing dick into her hot mouth "—having you deep inside of me. Then out of me. Then inside me." She worked him up and down, chasing her hand with her mouth, pulling him deeper and deeper with each steady suck.

Will gritted his teeth against the onslaught, locked his thighs to keep from pumping himself in and out of her mouth. He lay there, listened to her greedy mouth, jerked beneath her talented tongue until he thought for sure he'd explode.

"Enough," Will finally growled, unable to take anymore. Besides, he had something to prove. That he could give as well as he could take. He nudged Rowan onto her back, slid down her belly, parted her curls, then fastened his mouth onto her core.

She gasped, jerked beneath his mouth.

Will lapped at the tiny nub hidden at the crest of her sex, then licked a trail farther down, and pushed his tongue deeply inside her, then flicked it as fast as he could. She bucked beneath him, cried out, but Will refused to stop. He'd told her he wanted to sip up her release and he wasn't mov-ing out from between her legs until he'd lapped up every last drop of it. He continued to flutter his tongue inside her, then worked a finger against her clit, and pressed the pad of his thumb ever so gently against the tight rosebud of her bottom.

It was a risky move, he knew, but one that usually paid off. Rowan momentarily stilled, evidently unsure, but then sensation took over and she went *wild*. She bucked frantically beneath him. Her head thrashed from side to side, arched off the bed. Every muscle in her body went rigid.

"Oh, God," she screamed, her voice a long, guttural wail of release.

He felt her spasm around his tongue, laved up every bit of the sweet release. Unable to stand another minute outside of her body, Will snagged a condom from his bedside drawer, tore into the packet and quickly rolled it into place. She was still recovering when he moved back between her legs.

Pink exertion stained her cheeks. Her breathing was heavy, labored, and she flung an arm over her forehead. "That was— I never—" She smiled at him, seemingly impressed. "There are no words."

Will grinned. "I've got a couple."

"Oh?"

"Open up." And with that he sank into her. Pulled in a satisfying breath as he filled his lungs once more. He looked down and his gaze found hers. Saw wonder, need, happiness and something else, something just beyond his understanding. Sound receded once more and his chest filled with a light, fluttery feeling he'd never experienced before. Something sharp and sweet and akin to awe.

And in a moment of blind comprehending panic he realized what it was—he was falling in love with her. The idea momentarily paralyzed him. In love? he thought wildly. He couldn't be in love? He'd just met her. Barely knew her. How the hell could he be in love?

Rowan rocked suggestively beneath him, smiled up at him. *Dark brown hair fanned over a white pillow, mossy-green eyes, adorable dimple.* She was the picture of perfection. Flushed and lush. His.

He returned her grin, pushed himself more deeply inside her. Ah hell, so what if he'd only known her a few days. Semantics, Will told himself. Screw it. He wanted her. Would always want her.

"YOU CAN STAY, you know," Will told her hours later, after bouts of sex, then rest and then more sex. His voice sounded kind of rusty, unaccustomed to making the offer, and she found herself inexplicably touched.

But something had happened to her tonight, and she knew that if she didn't leave and get some much-needed perspective, she'd lose her tentative grasp on reality as she knew it and she'd be lost. To what, she wasn't quite sure yet. But the knowledge was here all the same.

Curiously, if they'd been at her house, she suspected that she wouldn't have minded spending the night in his arms. Would love to wake up with him.

But being here, in this house, felt too much like a dream she'd wanted for entirely too long—one she typically avoided—and by spending the night, she was afraid she'd set herself up for something that she'd never have. Ridiculous? Probably. But self-preservation had kicked in and rationale was no match for fight-or-flight.

She was spooked.

She was having feelings for Will Foster that simply defied reason when one considered how long they'd known each other. She'd been utterly overjoyed when he'd pulled that little thumb trick, had come until she thought her back would break beneath the strain of release.

But then he'd pushed into her, he'd stilled, the most curiously wondering look had come over his face…and something had happened in her chest. A light winging sensation had flitted from lung to lung, then pushed up her throat, forcing a small disbelieving laugh that had rung too much like an epiphany she didn't dare acknowledge, at least until she was in the relative safety of her own bed.

Will doodled a figure-eight on her upper arm, the motion at once erotic and lulling. "What do you say?"

Rowan winced. "I'd better pass. I look out for Ida, and I really wouldn't feel comfortable being away overnight without letting someone know."

That, too, was the truth. Not to mention she'd have to get in a couple of hours work. Rowan swallowed a dejected sigh. Listening to guys tug on their dongs after she'd just had this amazing, back-clawing sex was *not* what she wanted to do at all, but there it was. Her job. Her extra income. Her dwindling student loan debt and more assurance that she'd never have to sponge off her parents. Sometimes being a rational, practical adult truly sucked.

Will let go a small breath, seemed to accept her excuse for what it was. "Sure. I understand."

"I appreciate the offer, though." She curled closer to him, pressed a lingering kiss on his chest. "I can tell that's not an offer you extend frequently and I'm—" Rowan struggled to find the right word "—flattered."

"Well, you should be," he said, seemingly pacified. She lifted her head and watched him scowl adorably. His hair was mussed and the beginning of a nice hickey had formed beneath his collarbone. "I've never asked anyone to spend the night here before."

Rowan didn't move. "Never?"

He shook his head. "Never."

She waited a beat and when he didn't elaborate, she decided to press him.

"Why not?"

What made her so special? she wanted to know. Wanted him to tell her. He'd pulled the No Fishing sign down off the pond, so he couldn't very well complain if she cast her line out for a compliment or two.

Will hesitated, seemed to be grappling with some momentous decision. Finally, he expelled a breath, then rolled to face her. "Look, Rowan. I'm just going to lay it all out on the line here, okay?" His lips slid into a helpless smile and there was a nervous quality to that sexy baritone she'd never heard before. "It's the only way I know how to be. I say what I mean, I mean what I say. I detest games. I hate being manipulated."

She nodded. Those were excellent qualities, and quite honestly, they sounded reminiscent of many of her own principles.

"The reason that I've never asked anyone to spend the night here is because I've never trusted anyone enough to fall asleep beside them." His matter-of-fact gaze held hers. "I've known you for just a few days, and I felt it with you *instantly*." He reached out, slid a finger down the slope of her

cheek. "I don't know what it is about you, but...
Well, you just do it for me." His eyes were warm
and sticky, drawing her to him. "I think about you
all the time. I've been fascinated by you from the
first moment I heard your voice." A rueful laugh
bubbled up his throat. "I keep a perpetual hard-on.
Hell, we had sex in a friggin' *bathroom* today. I've
never had in-public sex, or phone sex. Those were
firsts, I can assure you. There's a level of intensity,
of trust that I can't explain, that I want to explore.
If I'm scaring you, then I'm sorry. That's not my
intention. I just— I just want you to know the way
I feel, that this is not some wild-wind fling. I want
to spend more time with you, see where this goes.
I want to follow where it leads, and honestly—"
he shrugged lightly, offered another crooked smile
"—I've got a good feeling about it. I also want you
to stop having phone sex with other guys. I know
I don't have a right, that it sounds presumptuous
and bossy." He blew out a breath. "But there it is.
I can't help it. The very idea makes me want to put
my fist through a wall."

Wow, Rowan thought, literally blown away. She
was touched, thrilled, ecstatic and flattered all at
once. Delight mushroomed in her chest. She was
also surprised at his honestly. Though really she
had no reason to be. Everything about their relationship had been astonishingly frank. Their racy

phone conversations speedily leaped to mind. It only made sense that a certain level of comfort had been achieved early on, otherwise they would have never progressed with such alarming rapidity. And they definitely had.

His smile slipped a fraction. "Come on, Rowan. Don't leave me hangin'. What do you think?"

Rowan cleared her throat, did her best to search for the right words. Finally, she found one that would sum everything he'd said up nicely, and which once again neatly avoided the phone sex issue. She felt her lips form a tentative smile, traced his heartbreakingly handsome face with her gaze. Hope sprouted in her breast. "Ditto."

13

"WELL, DORIS. What do you think so far?"

They were T-minus three days and counting. Rowan had worked tirelessly on Doris's garden, so much so that he'd begun to notice dark smudges beneath her eyes. Of course, he was probably partially to blame for that as well, Will thought with a small grin.

Though she'd still not spent the entire night with him, he'd nevertheless kept her up late over the past week and a half. While he didn't completely buy the Ida-excuse, Will knew better than to press her. Things were going too damned great and he didn't want to do anything to rock the boat. Couldn't risk it.

Instead, he'd *adjusted*—married friends had explained the merit of adjusting—and though he knew it was wrong, he couldn't help but be proud of himself, because, quite frankly, adjustments of any sort seemed contrary to his nature. He made decisions, everyone else fell in line.

Nevertheless, to be more accommodating—because he was such a sweet person and had no ulterior motive hidden in his selfish little heart—he'd left his own bed and spent several nights with her—every night that she'd asked as a matter of fact.

To his eternal mortification, he waited with bated breath every evening to see if she'd invite him to stay. He'd learned that there was no rhyme or reason to her decision and reading her mood was pointless. She was always happy to see him, always eager to share her bed…just not always for the night.

Her mattress wasn't as comfortable as his, but having her sweet bottom snugged against his groin and her delightful breast in his hand while he slept more than made up for it. If Will had ever been happier, he couldn't recall it. His gaze slid to the author of his present joy. She was across the lawn, hanging another one of her whirligig pieces, which Doris had picked out, on a newly planted weeping willow tree.

She'd twisted her long hair into a big, messy bun and had anchored it to the back of her head with a couple of chopsticks. Will frowned. At least, he supposed they were chopsticks, but hell who knew? He didn't keep up with women's hair fashions. All he knew was that he loved her hair. He let go an unsteady breath.

Particularly when she was balancing on his dick, with her neck arched back where it brushed the tops of his thighs.

Or when she leaned forward and kissed him, and it formed a veil around the side of his face.

Or when it slithered coolly over his chest. A hell of an aphrodisiac, her hair, Will thought with a silent sigh.

"Will?" Doris said, her exasperated tone indicating that she'd tried unsuccessfully to garner his attention. She twinkled her fingers in his face. *"Will."*

He blinked. "Er…sorry. Yes, Doris?"

"I said that I'm in love with my garden, and—" her faded blue eyes twinkled with perceptive humor "—if I'm not sadly mistaken, you're in love with someone *in* my garden," she added with a wry smile.

There was that phrase again, Will thought.

In love.

Truth be told, it had strolled in and out of his brain several times recently, at the most curious moments. Last week, he'd watched her accidentally smear dirt on her face while transplanting a begonia, and a wave of affection had hit him so hard a lump had inexplicably formed in his throat.

Then today, he'd caught her chewing her nail, a thoughtful frown worrying her brow as she tried to figure out exactly where to place Doris's patio set, and the same unnerving sensation had taken hold. Something warm and light had moved into his chest, pushed into his throat, forced him to swallow.

It was the little things, Will realized now. Those small, insignificant little details that somehow added up until he knew he had the perfect person. The perfect partner.

Will shot Doris a look, didn't bother trying to deny it. He shrugged. "What can I say? She's one helluva woman."

Doris readily agreed. "She's fantastic, Will. She suits you. And she's tremendously talented. I think she could bring some much-needed whimsy to your business. Not everybody likes traditional landscaping. Look at me," she offered lightly, as though she hadn't been the bane of his professional existence for three *excruciating* years. "I'm the perfect example."

Will muffled a snort, inclined his head. He shifted, pushed a hand through his hair.

"What does your mother think about her?"

"Mom loves her, thinks she's the greatest thing since sliced bread."

Of course she would, Will thought, because just as he'd predicted his mother had taken one look at them together and deduced the obvious. She'd welcomed Rowan as part of the family without the smallest hesitation, and just yesterday he'd caught her on the phone with a friend who worked at Sylvia Gardens discussing available dates for the Chester-Hollings House, a popular wedding spot in downtown Jackson.

Truth be told, he'd always imagined getting married at the botanical garden. It was gorgeous, a favorite haunt of his. He'd donated countless hours to helping maintain it. Cram-packed with hundreds of naturalized bulbs and perennials, azaleas, camellias and daylilies, the garden changed dramatically from season to season, and in certain grottos, from sunrise to sunset even. Hundreds of songbirds claimed sanctuary there, making it a gorgeous place to hold a wedding.

Rowan strolled over to stand beside him, wiped a hand across her brow, inadvertently streaking dirt across her face. Unable to help himself, he smiled as affection welled within him, then slung an arm over her shoulder, and tugged her closer to him. "You've done a fantastic job," he told her, making sure that she heard the admiration in his tone.

In fact, in appreciation, he'd already planned a special celebration for the conclusion of Doris's project. In addition to wining and dining her, great sex and hopefully more great sex, Will intended to ask her to come to work with him permanently.

Doris was right. Rowan had a lot to offer and his company would undoubtedly flourish as a result of her expertise. Foster's Landscape Design needed her, almost as desperately as he did.

"Thanks," Rowan murmured. Her assessing gaze scanned the yard and he had the privilege of watching pride slowly dawn in those gorgeous green eyes, watched her shoulders sag with the accomplishment of a job well done. She'd literally transformed Doris's backyard and it had turned out so much better than either one of them had hoped for. One thing was for certain, his satisfaction-guaranteed record was definitely safe...even if his heart wasn't.

"I was just telling Will here that he should consider—"

"—taking you to lunch," Will finished with a telling glare at Doris. Damn. Couldn't he have a single secret? He nudged her toward his truck. "You are hungry, right?"

Her eyes twinkled. "I could eat. I'm in the mood for something...salty but sweet," she finished, her voice loaded with innuendo.

Will knew exactly what she was talking about and the mere knowledge engulfed his loins in a flash-fire of heat. The image of her lips wrapped around his rod, sucking him until he came hard materialized behind his lids, instantly pushing his dick up behind his zipper.

Will let go a stuttering breath. "I think a trip to the pool hall's in order."

Rowan grinned and her eyes twinkled with equal amounts of heat and humor. "Ah…another psychic deduction."

"I'M NOT SO SURE about this," Rowan said hesitantly as Will fastened a blindfold over her eyes.

"What's there not to be sure of? You trust me, don't you?"

Implicitly, Rowan thought. She truly did. Didn't even have to think about it.

The past couple of weeks with Will had been the most memorable—most pleasurable—of her life. Simply being with him, feeling him unexpectedly sliding his hand into hers, or a tender kiss on her cheek, not to mention those more intimate moments—feeling him inside her, the frantic race for release when nothing existed beyond the exquisite sensation of their joined bodies—had to be the most incredible thing a girl could ever ask for. Did she trust him? Oh, she more than trusted him.

At some point, and she didn't know when precisely, she'd fallen head over heels in love with him.

The idea was singularly terrifying and if she didn't suspect that he felt every bit as strongly for her, she'd have undoubtedly headed for higher ground already. But there was something inexplicably sweet about the way he looked at her, a softer emotion she so desperately wanted to trust, to believe in.

Unfortunately, there was a small part of her that couldn't quite surrender to the feeling, and that part kept her from doing the one thing she knew he wanted her to do—spend the night. The issue would probably come up again this evening, and though she knew Will wouldn't press her, she dreaded it all the same.

She knew that he didn't understand her reluctance, knew that he'd compromised by coming and spending the night with her, but Rowan also knew that one night in this old farmhouse would be all it took for her to be firmly—irrevocably—attached to him and that happily ever after dream that had become brighter and brighter with every moment that she spent with him.

His house had felt curiously like home from the instant she'd walked in the door—hell, she'd started redecorating within sixty seconds of crossing the threshold—and every additional minute spent under his roof, in his yard—with him—made her want it all the more keenly. She had to hang on to some sort of perspective and the only way she knew to maintain that was to go home and climb into her own bed. Crazy? Delusional? Insane? All of the above, but she didn't know what else to do.

She let him make love to her, she relished every second that they spent together, then she went home and stepped back into reality—a lonely bed and phone sex.

Quite honestly, she could face the lonely bed more easily than she could face her 1-900-line. Keeping that up had gotten increasingly harder. It had always been a quick way to make a buck, had never been anything more than a job, but now that she had some firsthand experience with the genuine article… Well, suffice it to say the very idea of pretending made her ill. And though she'd managed to avoid answering his questions about it, Rowan knew that he assumed that she'd quit. She'd made it a point to hide it from him, which she knew in her heart of hearts was wrong. Anything that she couldn't share didn't belong in their relationship. Which was why she'd called the phone company today and arranged to have the line disconnected at the end of the month. It was paid for until then.

Did she need the money? Yes. She could list a dozen plausible reasons why she could keep it, but only one reason to let it go—*Will*—and that one was enough. If she didn't get called back to school in the fall, then she'd simply find something else. Rowan smiled. Last she heard there was an opening at the Bag-A-Bargain. She'd rather work there for less money than have this funky sense of dishonesty hovering between them.

"Ah, I see that smile," Will told her. "I knew you'd come around. Careful now, watch your step." Will led her down a pair of steps and the sweet scent of roses instantly assailed her senses. So they were in his rose garden. Interesting.

"Tell me again what we're doing," Rowan asked, intrigued.

"We're playing a kinky little game I like to call Name That Smell. It involves a little light bondage and for every scent you correctly name, you get a reward." He drew her to a stop and let go a deep breath. "But first you have to get naked."

Rowan laughed out loud. "Light bondage? I don't remember agreeing to bondage."

"Oh, but you did. This afternoon when we were in the bathroom at Grady's again, I distinctly remember you telling me that I could have anything I wanted if I would just hurry up and fu—"

"Right," Rowan interrupted him, her face flushing with remembered heat and humiliation. She couldn't believe she'd said that, couldn't believe that he'd had her so damned desperate that she'd agreed to give him anything he wanted so long as he'd simply fill her up, put her out of her misery.

Though she couldn't see him, she knew beyond

a shadow of a doubt that he was grinning from ear to ear. "You're enjoying this entirely too much, Will."

He laughed. "What?" he asked innocently. "You were the one who said—"

"I know what I said," she interrupted. "I'm here and I'm ready."

"Willing, maybe," Will qualified. She felt him sidle closer to her, felt his fingers tug at the hem of her shirt. "But I don't know about ready. Luckily, I can help you with that."

A laugh stuttered out of her. "Oh, I'll just bet you can."

"Now, onto that naked part I told you about." She felt him move in behind her, draw her shirt up over her head. Her bare back landed again his bare chest, pushing a sizzling sigh from between her lips.

Rowan gasped. "When did you get naked?"

"I've been shedding clothes all the way out here." He paused. "In fact, I should probably go pick them up and put them in the hamper."

"Don't you dare," Rowan growled with a laugh.

Will chuckled, the wretch. "You're right." His hands slid up over her sides, came around and cupped her breasts through her bra. She sagged against him, let her head fall back on his shoulder. An erotic little thrill moved through her. Curiously, the blindfold heightened her other senses. The feel of his skin, the perfumed scent in the air. He popped the closure, freeing her nipples to the night, to his warm, skilled touch, then thumbed her, pulling another pleased sigh from between her smiling lips. "I've been thinking about this all day," he told her, his voice husky with desire. "Thinking about the moonlight against your naked skin and the scent of roses while I love you."

His hands slid down her belly, unfastened her shorts and ever so slowly, pushed them over her hips. Her wet panties swiftly followed. "God, you're beautiful. I know I've told you before, but I just can't say it enough. I look at you and…and sometimes I can't breathe."

Her heart warmed at the sincere compliment, along with other areas of her body. "I know that feeling," she told him. "It happens to me quite frequently when I look at you as well." And it did. He, too, was beautiful, just in a different way.

Will threaded his fingers through hers, tugged her deeper into his garden room, then helped her lie down on what she could only assume was a mattress…covered with rose petals. A smile inexplicably formed on her lips. A warm wall of hard male flesh moved into place beside her.

"Trite, I know," he whispered, sliding a petal slowly down her belly. "But it's always been a fantasy of mine."

Hers, too, and she didn't care that it was trite.

He'd done it for her, which made it incredibly special. "Mine, too," Rowan confessed. She rolled toward him, slid her arm around his waist and licked the hollow of his throat. "I'm…touched."

"Not nearly as much as you're about to be," Will warned with a sexy chuckle. "Which brings me to the light bondage point of our evening." She felt him move, evidently reaching for something, and the next instant, a vine of some sort looped around one of her wrists.

Rowan gasped. "What are you doing?"

"Weren't you listening? I'm tying you up. Your hands are…distracting. I want to touch you. Lick you. Kiss you. And you have to lie back and take it."

Oh, well, in that case… Rowan offered her other wrist up and chuckled. "Am I supposed to argue?"

"A token protest would be nice."

"Will, please," Rowan pleaded, stifling a laugh. "Please don't lick me, kiss me, worship me and make me lie back and take it. It's a torture I can't bear."

He chuckled, attached one wrist to the other. "Smart-ass."

"Hey, you're the one who made the rules. I'm simply going to enjoy them. What are you tying me up with?" A vine of some sort, but she couldn't tell which kind.

"Ivy," Will told her, finishing it up. "You're

lying in a bed of rose petals, bound with ivy, and completely at my mercy," he added. His mouth latched onto her breast, effectively pulling the air from her lungs. "What have you got to say about that?"

She laughed again. "Please don't throw me in the brier patch."

She felt a bloom of some sort drift over her belly, do a lazy figure eight around the globes of her breasts and a sigh eddied out of her mouth. She melted into the mattress, fully prepared to take this scene to whatever level he wanted. "Ah," Rowan sighed. "That feels nice."

"I've been thinking about doing this," he confided, his voice a decadent rumble. "Thinking about painting your body with flowers."

A steady throb commenced between her legs. "How about painting my body with kisses?"

"In time," he murmured, dragging the bloom over her thigh, then behind the bend of her knee, over the top of her foot. The delicate flower made the return trek, brushed her curls, then her nether lips, and another sibilant sigh hissed past her lips as sensation bolted through her. Her nipples budded even tighter, tingled. He was priming her, Rowan realized, purposely dragging out the tension, dallying because he knew it drove her wild.

"Will," she murmured, a desperate tone in her

voice that she recognized, knew he recognized as well.

"Yes?" She heard the smile in his voice, the triumph.

Rowan could have ranted and raved, could have cursed and begged—that's what she'd done this afternoon, what had put her in this position in the first place. The sheer unadulterated truth had worked before—seemed to be the only way they could communicate—so she opted for honesty.

"I need you." A simple entreaty, the whole truth.

He stilled, she could feel it, could feel the very atmosphere around them change. The night sounds became sharper, the scent keener, and her body literally vibrated with a need so intense, an emotion so true that she felt her eyes water behind the blindfold. She loved their sexy play, loved every instant of every moment they'd been together. But tonight, she wanted something different. Wanted to strip down barriers and revel in honest lovemaking. Wanted to lend truth to an act that she knew she couldn't share with another soul.

She felt Will's fingers at her wrists, felt the bonds give way and sag. Then, very gently, he pushed the blindfold away from her eyes. Will's handsome face loomed instantly into view. The pad of his thumb skimmed her bottom lip and those gorgeous honey eyes were rife with emotion, with a quiet intensity and understanding that made her want to weep. "I need you, too."

She looped her hands around his neck and lowered her voice. "Then love me. Just love me."

"I do, Rowan," he murmured softly.

Then he did.

14

WILL DISCONNECTED, clipped his phone back onto his shorts, then hurriedly slid behind the wheel of his truck. It was a little late to be making sure that their reservations were a go, but Will hadn't had time to check in with his mom. Things had been too crazy.

They'd finished up in Doris's yard today—she'd been thrilled, ecstatic, over the moon and this time the sentiment seemed to have stuck. She'd been beyond pleased with the way things had turned out, so much so that she'd added a sizable bonus to her already hefty check.

Will looked forward to giving it to Rowan— she'd earned it, after all—and he planned to hand it over, then offer her a permanent job. He also knew he'd be asking her another significant question in the not-too-distant future as well.

When she'd told him that she needed him the night before last, it was as though she'd inadvertently set the hook and reeled him in. He'd literally felt it—felt the bite, the jerk and the subsequent fall. He might have worried about it, too, had it not been for one thing.

She'd spent the night.

In his rose garden, under a blanket of stars and a hundred-year old quilt, utterly, deliciously naked, snuggled against him as though nothing else mattered in the world, so long as they could breathe the same air. And, though he couldn't be completely certain because the idea that he'd fallen in love— had actually trusted someone enough to make that leap—had just about fried his brain, he grimly suspected that he'd told her that he loved her.

In fact, was almost certain of it, and he imagined that confession was no small part of the reason she'd stayed with him. Whatever the reason, Will could only be grateful. She'd stayed with him every night since and he wanted her to stay every night from here on out. He wanted to be with her all the time, hated every second they were apart, and anticipated the time he knew they'd be together with the sort of reverent, expectant joy that could only be attributed to being madly in love with her. When had it happened? Will couldn't pinpoint an exact time, but if he had to guess, then he imagined he'd been on the slippery slope since the first instant he'd heard that incredible voice of hers.

Which brought to mind another perk—she'd

obviously quit answering her 900-line. Will had
told himself this for the past two weeks, purposely
lied to himself—he'd had to in order to keep from
going *insane* every time she left to go home—but
given what they'd shared night before last, he
knew her well enough to know that she couldn't
possibly still be doing it, not when things between
them had moved to such an intimate level. She
wouldn't betray him that way. Couldn't. She had
too much class, and he fully believed that she cared
just as much about him as he did about her.

Naturally a small part of Will wanted to question their good thing—a leftover habit from a bad
relationship—but he had too much respect for
Rowan to let the past ruin what he instinctively
knew could be a beautiful future.

She was forever material. That forever kind of
love that was constantly lauded in music and film,
the ultimate brass ring, and he fully intended to
reach for it.

For her.

But one thing at a time, Will told himself. He
pulled into Rowan's drive, slowed to a stop, and
shifted into Park. A quick glance at the dash told
him he was a little early—about thirty minutes to
be exact—but he simply hadn't been able to wait
to see her, to set tonight in motion.

He'd been waiting for two weeks to ask this

question, to essentially put their future on the right track, and waiting another few minutes was simply outside the realm of his control. He felt like an impatient kid with a nickel in his pocket at the penny-candy counter.

He wanted to ask her *now.*

Quite honestly, he'd planned to give her the check and make the offer during dinner, but he seriously didn't see himself being able to wait that long.

Will blew out a breath, exited the truck and made his way to her door. He could probably ask her on the way to the restaurant, then they could celebrate over dinner. Better yet, he could ask her now, and they could start celebrating even earlier. He smiled. The idea held considerable appeal, and gained momentum as he strolled up her steps.

Will lifted his hand to knock, but the sound of her laughter stopped him. A clammy sweat instantly broke out all over his body. He knew that laugh. He'd heard it the first day he'd met her, then had heard it several times since, only in those instances that sexy chuckle had been for him.

Will swallowed and something stark and painful cut through his chest. He didn't know what made him do it, didn't know what propelled him, but rather than knocking on the door, he opened it as quietly as he could and followed that tinkling sultry sound to the back of the house.

"Oh, that's positively wicked. I like the way your mind works." She sighed dramatically, the sound at once sexy and hurtful.

Will stopped in her hallway as she came into view. Rowan stood in front of her bathroom mirror, the bedamned headset in place over her ears. He silently swore, felt that newfound hope he'd just moments ago entertained wither and die like a forget-me-not planted in full sun. His hands fisted at his sides.

She wore a white lacy bra, matching panties and nothing else. Need instantly bombarded him, but he ruthlessly tamped it down. She leaned forward and applied some frosty-looking powder on one of her eyelids. Ordinarily, he would have been content to simply watch her. It was fascinating really, that she went to so much trouble to make herself beautiful, when all she had to do was breathe. But in the next instant he forgot about watching her for pleasure, and watched instead as a too familiar scene—one he'd witnessed two weeks ago— played out in front of his disbelieving eyes.

"Oh, Rick," she sighed. "You can't know how *hot* you're making me. Yes, yes, I know. Oh, I'm wearing a black teddy and spiked heels. No, no panties," she sighed. "I never wear panties. I like to be readily accessible, if you get my drift."

Will told himself that she was playing a part.

He plainly saw that. She was getting absolutely nothing out of this exchange. He reminded himself that she needed the money—that she didn't want to sponge off her parents the way her brother had, a tidbit she'd shared recently. He told himself all these things and, though he desperately wanted to laugh like he had the first time he'd seen her do this, Will found himself unable to conjure the necessary humor to complete this scene.

A thousand needles were stabbing into his chest and that near-suffocating sensation took hold, but for a completely different reason this time, he knew. His skin felt like it was going to split and the familiar burn of humiliation and anger tore through like water bursting through a broken dam.

Will smirked as she rounded out her performance once more with another long ecstatic howl of feigned sexual gratification. He was a fool. An utter and complete fool. He didn't wait for her to finish her call this time, but rather lifted his hands and applauded. His hands smacked together, cracking through her small house like the gunfire.

She jumped and squealed and her startled eyes found his. "Will," she breathed.

"Sorry I interrupted," Will told her. "It's a bad habit, but one I'm committed to breaking. I swear it'll never happen again." And it wouldn't. His mind black with hurt and rage, he turned abruptly on his heel and headed for the door.

He heard Rowan call after him, heard her shout his name, but he was too upset to heed her, too caught up in his own stupidity to listen to anything she had to say.

God, he'd been an idiot.

Again.

He heard her screen door bang open as he reached his truck. "Will, *wait!*" she pleaded. "Please let me explain! I'm sorry, I just—" She drew up short. *"Please."*

Will squeezed his eyes tightly shut and his hand hesitated on the car door. God, he wanted to. Wanted to wait and hear her out. He pulled in a harsh breath, waited while pride battled need, battled reason and hope. But reason and hope had won once to a disastrous outcome and this time pride simply wouldn't concede defeat. Though he felt like he was coming apart at the seams, Will jerked the door open, started the truck and shot out of her drive.

Out of her life.

ROWAN WATCHED Will tear out of drive and felt her heart threaten to explode right out of her chest. Her breath came in sharp, painful gasps and a silent sob formed in the back of her throat.

One look into those devastated brown eyes and she'd felt her own heart break. She'd heard him clap, then she'd turned around and... And that worst enemy mask of his had fallen firmly into place, that damaged smile, so much so that Rowan sincerely doubted she'd ever be able to make him listen to her, make him understand.

Oh, shit.

What had she done? What the hell had she done? Panic crowded her throat, threatened to strangle her. She turned and walked blindly back into her house, pushed a shaky hand through her hair. She muttered a stream of obscenities, paced back and forth in front of her couch, too wired and frightened to sit. She couldn't blame him for being hurt, for being mad. Were the situation reversed, she'd undoubtedly feel the same way.

Oh, God, Rowan silently wailed. Why the hell hadn't she disconnected that damned line? Why had she answered that ignorant call? Because she was an idiot, she thought with a bitter laugh. Because so long as she was paying to have the damned thing, she might as well answer the line. She was too damned practical for her own good, and look at what it had possibly cost her. Will's parting comment ricocheted through her cramping brain.

I swear it'll never happen again.

He couldn't mean what she thought, Rowan

thought faintly. He couldn't mean that they were finished. The mere thought terrified her, made her belly tip in a nauseated roll. Surely not. Surely he'd give her the opportunity to explain. He'd have to, Rowan decided. She'd make him. She knew that his ex had done a number on him, knew that she'd played him for a fool, and though Rowan knew she'd made a terrible mistake, she hadn't done either of those things. Would never purposely try to hurt him. She swallowed, felt the burn of impending tears scald the backs of her eyes.

She loved him.

He had to know it. And if he didn't, then she'd enlighten him. The perfect way to do that rose like cream to the top of her churning brain, and she stilled, calmed by the presence of a plan. She knew exactly what to do, Rowan decided. The trouble would be getting him to go along with it.

WILL PULLED a beer from the fridge, then made his way to the living room. Though he wasn't remotely interested in watching television, he turned it on anyway. The noise pushed the quiet away, which helped push his thoughts away. He didn't want to think—thinking depressed him.

Truth be told he'd like nothing better than to get blind, roaring drunk, but drowning his troubles in alcohol had never been his thing and he wasn't about to start now. His gaze landed on the phone and he had to force himself to look away. Had to force himself to keep from picking it up and calling her. If he could only hear her voice...

Will swore at the pathetic thought. Her voice was what had gotten him into this mess, his insatiable need to hear her, to be with her. He swallowed. To make love to her. The memory of her greedy body clenching around him, the perfect taste of her pearled nipple on his tongue momentarily took hold of him, making an ache start deep in his chest and infect every cell in his body.

God he wanted her.

Was it really so important to be right? Will wondered now. Was it worth the agony of being alone? Of being without her?

Quite frankly, he suspected that he'd overreacted, that he should have let her explain like she'd asked to do, but having been screwed so royally once before, Will couldn't trust his instincts, couldn't decide if it was truly the case or wishful thinking on his part. And as much as he wanted her, he didn't want to be a fool. Couldn't allow it.

His gaze slid to the phone once more. Which meant that, no matter how much he might want to, he flatly refused to call her. And to his immeasurable disquiet and surprise, she hadn't called him either. Two days had passed without a word, and though he was loath to admit it, it was absolutely killing him. He felt dead on the inside, unable to breathe. Numb and joyless. It was awful.

He'd been humiliated by his ex, that was for sure, but he'd realized something over the past couple of days that he'd never realized before— he hadn't been in love with her. There'd been a sense of relief when they'd split up, one Will instinctively knew he'd never feel about the breakup with Rowan.

The shriek of his phone ringing rose above the din of the TV and Will cursed the instant leap of hope that jumped into his chest. Rowan? he always wondered. Every time the line had rung, his first thought had been her. Hell, who was he trying to kid. *Every* thought was of her.

Irritated with himself, Will refused to answer it, refused to check the Caller ID display. His machine picked up, then her achingly familiar voice—the one he'd desperately been waiting to hear—sounded.

"Will, hi," she said tentatively. "Look, I know I don't deserve it, but I would really like the chance to talk to you. To explain," she said haltingly. "I know it's going to sound strange, and I know I have no right to ask…but I'd really appreciate it if you'd do something for me. Call this number—" To his astonishment, she rattled off her 900-number. "In a few minutes, I'll give you a call back. If you don't answer, then I'll leave you alone." He heard her swallow. "I'll, uh… I'll never bother you again. But things were pretty special between us—at least for me—and I'm hoping that you'll at least give me the benefit of the doubt."

She hung up.

Will sat there for a moment, silently considered what she said. Tried to pretend like the fact that she'd called, or that she'd sounded every bit as miserable as he felt didn't matter.

But it did.

His first impulse was to ease her pain, to let her know that he cared that she ached, that he ached, too, and in that moment he knew that he'd do whatever she asked, he'd believe whatever she told him, because he desperately wanted her back, wanted to be with her, and his pride could go to hell. His need for control could go to hell.

He wanted her. Had to have her.

He blew out a breath, picked up the phone and dialed her 900-line and to his complete bewilderment, he got a recorded message saying that the line had been disconnected, was no longer in service.

His heart began to race and a small seed of hope sprouted once more in the fallow field of his chest. Did this mean— Could she have—

The line rang again, and this time Will didn't

hesitate to answer. He cleared his throat of some nebulous obstruction. "Hello."

"Will." The word was drenched in relief.

He rubbed the bridge of his nose, felt that sweet sultry voice seep into him. Felt the backs of his eyes burn. "Yeah?"

"I'm sorry."

Two words. That was all it took for him to literally shake with an emotion so strong it was all he could do not to weep. "No," he sighed. "I'm sorry. I was unreasonable. I—"

"No you weren't," she interrupted. "You were right to be angry, had every right to be mad. I don't blame you. I just—" She expelled a soft breath. "I'd planned on turning it off at the end of the month. I couldn't do it anymore, hated it after being with you." A frustrated growl issued from her throat. "I'm an idiot. I can't offer an excuse that's good enough and the only one I have sounds lame even to me. I was paying for it, so I thought I should answer it. See?" she told him, clearly irritated. "It's stupid. I don't expect you to understand—that's fine—I just wanted you to know that it's off, and I guess what I'm asking is if you can... If you can forgive me? Can we get past this? Because I really want to." She drew up short, let go a soft breath that made his fingers involuntarily curl. "I miss you. I want you to hold me and kiss me and make love to me. I want to fall asleep in your arms. I want to grow things together. A garden, flowers…kids." She stopped again, her voice cracking. "I just want you, what I think we can have."

For a moment Will couldn't speak, couldn't move. He absorbed everything that she said, felt it creep into his chest and take root.

She made a nervous sound, like a sob caught in the back of her throat. "Well, I guess that's my answer. Sorry to have bothered you. Bye—"

"Rowan, wait!"

"Yeah?" she asked hesitantly.

"Everything you said, about being together and growing things." He swallowed. "Well…ditto."

Another sound, part-laugh, part-cry came through the line, pushing his lips up into a relieved smile. God how he missed her. How he needed her. He couldn't breathe without her. Had to have her.

"I think that you should come over," he told her, desperate to be with her once more.

A knock sounded at his door. "I think that you should open the door."

Will felt another slow smile slide across his lips. He stood and, phone still in hand, calmly made his way to the door and pulled it open. Rowan stood on the other side, an adorable grin on her lush, ripe mouth. His heart inexplicably swelled…as did another equally impatient organ in his lower extremities. He let his gaze trace the woefully familiar shape of her face. "I love you," he murmured softly.

Her eyes misted, searched his. "I love you, too."

Will tossed his phone aside, stepped forward and crushed her to him. She sighed, melted against him.

Then he kissed her…and could breathe again.

Epilogue

Two months later...

"COME ON," Will cajoled, steering his new wife determinedly away from well-wishers. "I'm ready to go."

"Me, too," she told him, the heat in that sultry nonwhisper the only proof that he needed that she was every bit as impatient as him to leave. "But we can't be rude."

"Yes you can," Alexa said. "It's the prerogative of newlyweds. No one expects you to hang around after the reception." Her eyes sparkled, and she lifted another glass of champagne in their honor. "I *predict* that no one will mind."

Rowan grinned. "I predict that you're full of sh—"

"Careful," Will interrupted, laughing. "We're in mixed company, remember?"

Will's nephew, Scott, ambled up once more, shot her a curious look. "Are you sure we haven't met? There's something so familiar about you. I feel like I've talked to you before."

Rowan and Will shared a look. Scott had been trying to place her for weeks now and, though Will knew Rowan fervently prayed he never figured it out, Will couldn't help but be tickled by the whole scenario.

"Er...I don't think so," Rowan told him again, her standard answer. Scott scratched his head, shot her another baffled look as though he wanted to argue, then reluctantly walked away.

Rowan sagged against him, her soft breast branding his arm. "Geez, that's nerve-racking. Do you think he'll ever figure it out?" she hissed.

Will smiled down at her. "I don't know. But, like you said, he's pretty bright."

She scowled adorably. "Oh, shut up."

Will pulled a wounded look. "We've been married an hour and you're already bossing me around? Should I be worried?"

Her eyes twinkled with humor and heat. "Definitely."

Will bent his head and kissed her. That lush mouth melded to his effortlessly and within seconds he was so damned hot that self-combustion became a genuine fear. His dick strained against his tux, tenting his cummerbund out in the most undignified fashion.

She chuckled against his mouth. "I want you.

Right now. What do you say we find a private little grotto and I'll show you just how much." She lowered her voice. "Repeatedly."

"Get a room!" someone shouted, before Will could reply. His brother, no doubt, Will thought, dragging his lips reluctantly from hers. He rested his forehead against hers and they shared a smile. Happiness saturated every pore of his body.

"I take it you're ready to blow this shindig?" he asked softly. This shindig was costing a fortune, but he didn't care. He'd rented Sylvia Gardens, had spared absolutely no expense. He only intended to get married once and to that end, he'd made sure that everything had been done right, to Rowan's specific instructions.

His heart squeezed painfully in his chest as he looked at her now. Just a few months ago, he'd imagined her like this. Long white gown, a garland of flowers in her hair, and here they were, happier than he ever thought they could possibly be.

"I'm ready when you are," she told him in that too-sultry near-whispering voice. "If you're sure your mother won't be hurt that we leave early."

Will grinned. "She'll get over it," he said drolly. In fact, she'd given him another one of those embarrassing talks yesterday, and had informed him in no uncertain terms that a grandchild was expected posthaste. He was now at liberty to forgo the condoms. Did he have any questions? As if he didn't know how to go about getting his wife pregnant.

Sheesh, Will thought. He thought he could handle *that* without any damned motherly pearls of wisdom. To that end, he made a mental note to leave his phone at home. He didn't want any unsolicited advice on how to conduct his honeymoon.

She sighed softly and those gorgeous green eyes tangled with his. Love, joy, and need shimmered in those mesmerizing orbs, causing his chest to inexplicably tighten.

Will laced his fingers through hers, then whistled loudly to garner everyone's attention. "We're leaving," he said without preamble. "Enjoy the party."

This abrupt announcement was met with laughter and applause. Smiling, they both turned and made their way to Rowan's car. She'd threatened bodily injury to anyone who touched her baby, so there were no cans tied to the bumper, or a Just Married scrawled in shoe polish across the windshield.

She stopped next to the passenger side and calmly waited for him to open the door, as though this were completely normal and nothing out of the ordinary was happening.

Will stilled, then shot her a questioning look. His heart began to pound, to race. "Rowan?"

She smiled, then turned and winked at her dad,

who beamed at them and sent her a quiet thumbs-up. Her gaze slid back to Will, then, and she tossed him the keys. "Second sticks a little," she said matter-of-factly, "so you might want to baby her."

Will swallowed, recognizing the gesture for what it was. She trusted him. Fully, completely, without reservation. "Are you sure?" he asked, his throat tight.

She smiled at him and liquid emotion glittered in those gorgeous green eyes. She pulled a light shrug, laughed. "What can I say? I finally found a guy who's vintage-Vette worthy." She swallowed. "I love you, Will."

Will grinned. "Ditto."

Blaze

HARLEQUIN® Blaze™

Falling Inn Bed...

**One night between the sheets here
changes everything!**

Join author

Jeanie London

as she takes you to the hottest couples'
resort around. In this resort's sexy theme
rooms, anything can happen when
two people hit the sheets.

Read how falling in bed can lead to falling in love with

October 2004 **HOT SHEETS #153**
November 2004 **RUN FOR COVERS #157**
December 2004 **PILLOW CHASE #161**

Don't miss these red-hot stories
from Jeanie London!

Look for these books at your favorite retail outlet.

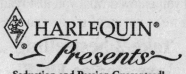

HARLEQUIN®
Presents

Seduction and Passion Guaranteed!

INTERNATIONAL DOCTORS

**They're guaranteed
to raise your pulse!**

Meet the most eligible medical men in the world in a
new series of stories by popular authors that
will make your heart race!

Whether they're saving lives or dealing with desire,
our doctors have bedside manners that send
temperatures soaring....

Coming December 2004:

The Italian's Passionate Proposal
by Sarah Morgan

#2437

Also, don't miss more medical stories
guaranteed to set pulses racing.

Promotional Presents features the
Mediterranean Doctors Collection in May 2005.

Available wherever Harlequin books are sold.

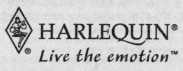

HARLEQUIN®
Live the emotion™

www.eHarlequin.com

HPINTDOC

If you enjoyed what you just read,
then we've got an offer you can't resist!

Take 2 bestselling
love stories FREE!
Plus get a FREE surprise gift!

Clip this page and mail it to Harlequin Reader Service®

IN U.S.A.	IN CANADA
3010 Walden Ave.	P.O. Box 609
P.O. Box 1867	Fort Erie, Ontario
Buffalo, N.Y. 14240-1867	L2A 5X3

YES! Please send me 2 free Blaze™ novels and my free surprise gift. After receiving them, if I don't wish to receive anymore, I can return the shipping statement marked cancel. If I don't cancel, I will receive 4 brand-new novels each month, before they're available in stores! In the U.S.A., bill me at the bargain price of $3.99 plus 25¢ shipping and handling per book and applicable sales tax, if any*. In Canada, bill me at the bargain price of $4.47 plus 25¢ shipping and handling per book and applicable taxes**. That's the complete price and a savings of at least 10% off the cover prices—what a great deal! I understand that accepting the 2 free books and gift places me under no obligation ever to buy any books. I can always return a shipment and cancel at any time. Even if I never buy another book from Harlequin, the 2 free books and gift are mine to keep forever.

150 HDN DZ9K
350 HDN DZ9L

Name	(PLEASE PRINT)	
Address	Apt.#	
City	State/Prov.	Zip/Postal Code

Not valid to current Harlequin Blaze™ subscribers.

Want to try two free books from another series?
Call 1-800-873-8635 or visit www.morefreebooks.com.

* Terms and prices subject to change without notice. Sales tax applicable in N.Y.
** Canadian residents will be charged applicable provincial taxes and GST.
  All orders subject to approval. Offer limited to one per household.
  ® and ™ are registered trademarks owned and used by the trademark owner and or its licensee.

BLZ04R   ©2004 Harlequin Enterprises Limited.